She was no longer merely a pretty girl dressed in black leather, but a radiant goddess whose clothes were a shimmering sheath of scarlet and gold. He was being torn apart by the frenzy of his desire for her, but Isis regarded him with the same indifference she might show to a worm. And still in his seat, by some magic he could feel the satin smoothness of her skin beneath his fingers and against his lips, while his nostrils avidly drank in her odour, honeyed yet raunchy, which proclaimed her triumphant sexuality . . .

By the same author

*The Happy Hooker*
*Letters to the Happy Hooker*
*Xaviera!*
*The Best Part of a Man*
*Xaviera's Supersex*
*Xaviera Goes Wild!*
*Xaviera Meets Marilyn Chambers* (with Marilyn Chambers)
*Knights in the Garden of Spain*
*Xaviera's Magic Mushrooms*
*Madame l'Ambassadrice*
*The Inner Circle*
*Lucinda, My Lovely*
*Fiesta of the Flesh*
*Lucinda: Hot Nights on Xanthos*
*Happily Hooked* (with John Drummond)
*Yours Fatally!*
*The Kiss of the Serpent*
*Let's Get Moving* (with John Drummond)

XAVIERA HOLLANDER

# Prisoner of the Firebird

Book Three of the
*Golden Phallus of Osiris* trilogy

This edition published 1995
by Diamond Books
77–85 Fulham Palace Road
Hammersmith, London W6 8JB

First published by Grafton Books 1988



ISBN 0 261 66644 4

Printed and bound in Great Britain

Set in Times

# Contents

# Part I
# Foreplay

# 1
## *Bedtime Story*

In the salon of his Paris apartment, Louis Halevy finished clearing away such debris as glasses, ashtrays and magazines – and the blood-drenched rug on which, a few hours earlier, Asi Moriba, the former tyrant of the African state of Salamba had been gunned down. The ivory wallpaper was splattered and streaked and the woodwork of the window was shattered where the fatal bullet had finally lodged. He tidied what he could, but there was no detergent or bleach which could dispel the stench of death.

Petra made her own preparations in the bedroom. She was a tall, athletic girl in her twenties who had enrolled in the Sorbonne where she was a student of Halevy, the Professor of Egyptology in the university. However, in their more intimate moments since she had moved into his flat, she had been able to reverse their roles and to give a few lessons to her teacher. It was one of those hot, sultry nights, not so much romantic as downright sexy, and Petra, perhaps stimulated by the day's drama, was in the mood to continue Louis' course of physical education. She had just emerged from a fragrant bath and her body was glowing and eager. She sprayed droplets of a musky, exotic perfume on those spots her lover most enjoyed nuzzling and she carefully selected a gauzy mauve nightdress since she knew that Louis found her more provocative when she wore the wisp of nylon which emphasized rather than hid the full richness of her breasts and the flowing contours of her hips.

'Put on some dreamy music and come to bed, Louis,' she called.

'I shan't be a minute.' he replied. 'I want to put our spare penis in the safe.'

'No, bring it into the bedroom, darling. I feel that it will spur you on to bigger and better things,' Petra laughed, but her gaiety barely disguised the panic which had assailed her when Milos, the revolutionary leader who had become the President of Salamba, had burst into the apartment and killed his rival.

'I must keep it under lock and key,' he protested. 'Hasn't it caused enough mischief for one day? The damned thing seems to drive men mad!'

'Just this once,' she pleaded. 'Tomorrow you can put it in the deepest vault of the biggest bank in Paris. But for tonight, let it be ours.'

Louis Halevy shrugged his shoulders in resignation, picked up the long, thick rod of gold and carried it into the bedroom.

'There you are, madam,' he smiled. 'For you alone, the Golden Phallus of Osiris.'

As he undressed, Petra ran her fingers over the shining metal as if to pluck from it the secret of its power to inspire men and women to the wildest excesses of lust and violence.

'Louis,' she whispered, 'I was so frightened. Not for me, darling; I thought that Moriba was going to kill you.'

'It was not me he was threatening,' Halevy pointed out grimly.

'With a madman like Moriba, nobody was safe.'

Petra dimmed the lights and the plaintive melody of one of the Liszt 'Années de Pèlerinage' stole into the room. Louis climbed between the crisp sheets and snuggled close to Petra. For a few minutes, they simply held each other, relaxing in the release from the terrors and tensions of the day. But seduction was in the air and when Louis tenderly kissed Petra's lips, she responded avidly.

Although the professor was some twenty years older than his student, her sexuality restored his golden youth and they made love in perfect harmony. As he fondled her taut, dark nipples, she felt those tiny tingles run through her, as if his hands were charged with electricity. Her tongue was thrusting deep into the cavern of his mouth, inviting him to plunge his insistent shaft into the warm, moist mysteries of her aching cunt and seal their bodies together. She arched her back and sighed with pleasure as he slid farther and farther in between the fleshy lips of her unresisting vagina. The sensation of being engulfed by her femininity always excited him, but on this night he experienced a greater intensity than he had ever known. He remembered the sheer wonder of the very first time that he had sunk inside a woman, and yet somehow this evening it was even better. He moved gently and slowly up and down and Petra raised her legs until she was able to cross them behind his neck, opening herself as wide as she could, as though she would be able to swallow up the whole of her man and hold him entrapped for ever inside her. Louis gripped her buttocks, plump and ripe as tropical fruit, and his head swam as he greedily inhaled the sweet and salt scent of her flowing love juices mingled with her perfume. His fine, proud penis swelled with desire and he felt the familiar tightening of his testicles which preceded his orgasm.

Petra divined the point to which his passion had progressed and played one of her favourite tricks, cruel and kind at the same time.

'No, not yet,' she breathed. 'First, give me your tongue.'

She pushed against his shoulders and at the same time her muscles contracted, easing him out remorselessly, despite his protests which they both knew were mere formalities. Leaving her was a sweet torment: he ached for the relief which had been denied him, but Petra had her needs and he knew well enough how to satisfy them. He moved himself down her body, savouring the soft, yielding flesh of her breasts and her belly, pausing to place his tongue into the inviting hollow of her navel. Then he wandered through the enchanted web of silky hairs which enticed him still lower until his face rested between her soaked thighs and he tenderly kissed her scarlet, swollen clitoris.

'Your tongue,' she repeated. 'You know the way I like you to do it.'

But now it was his turn to make her wait. Lifting her gently, he licked and sucked first at her brimming cunt and then stuck his tongue deep up her hot, tight arse. That was something which always turned her on, and she twisted and turned, moaning and sighing with an animal delight. As for Louis, he adored the sensation of his face being absolutely drenched by her tangy juices and of her toes playing with his rock-hard penis. But it was her clitoris which was clamouring for attention and it refused to wait, so she dropped her hand and started to masturbate herself furiously.

Gently but firmly, Louis Halevy removed her hand and let his tongue flick rapidly over her clitoris. Petra gasped and squirmed as if she wanted to escape but her lover played more and more purposefully over, under, around and across the tiny finger of sensitive flesh until he felt the muscles of her thighs tighten. She held his head in a grip as firm as a vice and her hands pushed his harder against her until that magic moment when the whole of her body trembled and she was consumed in a great, throbbing ecstasy. Her hands relaxed and she moved him away from her while her body went limp.

Halevy knew that it would only be a minute before she

recovered and the sensitiveness wore off: he had learned enough of the game of love to be patient, so he massaged his aching, unsatisfied cock until she was ready for him. For a while Petra lay back without moving, breathing deeply with her eyes tight closed. Louis Halevy raised himself until he was lying level with her and kissed her shoulders. She stirred as though she were waking from a deep sleep and with a purr of contentment reached out for his penis which she stroked. Suddenly she was wide awake and turned her back on him. But he knew that this was not a rejection but an invitation and easing her legs apart, he penetrated her from behind easily and deeply. With his hands clasping her breasts, he drove fiercely into her and she heaved the firm flesh of her buttocks back to meet his thrusts.

'Harder, give it all to me,' she coaxed.

He did not need encouragement. Every time he pulled away, it was as though he were dragged back by an irresistible force. The music was still playing in the salon, but all that Halevy could hear was the pounding of the blood in his head. The world was spinning round him but Petra was the constant centre of his universe and then he was wildly pumping his seed into her, or was it that she was sucking every last drop, drinking in his masculinity, draining from him the very essence of his life and leaving him shattered and exhausted but utterly fulfilled.

They lay close together for a long time without moving or speaking while the silvery tones of the piano concluded its serenade. At last he stirred like one returning from the land of the dead.

'That was fantastic,' he murmured.

Petra smiled, her eyes shining with satisfaction, and she found that without realizing what she had been doing, she had taken hold of the Golden Phallus and was tenderly stroking it. She shook her head in wonderment.

'Look, Louis,' she said. 'Do you think there can be any truth in all those strange stories about this thing?'

Halevy propped himself up on one elbow and wrinkled his nose in a thoughtful grin as he joined his hand to hers, gripping the chunky metal.

'Men say that when Seth, the Evil One, slew the Great God, Osiris, he hacked his body into thirteen parts and buried them in all the quarters of the globe. But Isis, mourning for the death of her husband, travelled the world until she had recovered all of them and by her magic reunited them. Only the phallus of her beloved evaded her and remained buried where, by its immense sexual potency, to this day it brings forth crops from the earth every year. And this object which you are fondling is the missing part of a magnificent golden statue, a replica in every respect of the body of the mythical god, so by such accounts it should be the most potent sexual symbol the world has ever known.'

'Yes, darling. I have attended all your lectures,' Petra interposed patiently. 'What I am asking is, do you believe there is any real basis for the superstition that this relic has occult sexual powers?'

'I think that if enough people have faith, whether it be in the efficacy of a magic charm or of a miracle, they make it come true,' Halevy replied, in the measured tones of the rational academic rather than those of the fervent lover.

'In that case,' Petra pointed out, 'you must have immense faith, judging by the way you have just performed.'

'Let's go to sleep,' Halevy suggested.

'What tact! What modesty!' laughed Petra.

She turned out the light and gently kissed him good night. Maybe it was her imagination, but as she turned on her side and gazed at where she had laid the Golden Phallus, she got the impression that there was another living presence in the room and a faint glow where there ought to have been darkness.

# 2
## *Sperm Bank*

The girl was wearing black leather, a cute jacket and a skirt which clung to her hips like a lover, and her looks were so sensational that even the most stolid of the good Swiss citizens who were passing by swivelled their heads round to gape at her. She was rather taller than the plump housewives carrying their bulging shopping baskets who gazed enviously at her exotically dusky complexion, marvelling how it could be so flawless and free from pimples in such striking contrast to their own. There was a rhythm to the curves of her body, her eyes were a vivid blue and her hair which brushed her shoulders was a sparkling, chestnut cataract.

The homely matrons wondered what such an apparition of beauty was doing in this part of their city, for the Paradeplatz in the heart of Zurich is a stately square, flanked by the heavy, stone buildings which house some of the world's most important banks and the girl seemed as out of place as a bird of paradise in a supermarket.

Not that she appeared to be overawed by her surroundings. She pushed her way through the heavy, glass door of the most imposing of the banks with all the self-assurance of an empress entering her domain. A dazzled porter hurried to ask if he could help her.

'Take me to Dr Josef Grunwald,' she demanded.

'I am sorry, madam,' the porter replied, shaking his head. 'Herr Grunwald cannot be disturbed. There is a meeting of the board of directors of the bank in progress, and Herr Grunwald is present.'

If he expected the girl to be impressed by this statement, he was disappointed. She looked at him coolly and produced a visiting card which she handed to him.

'Give that to Dr Grunwald at once,' she ordered.

'But I have explained, it is impossible to interrupt the meeting.'

'Do as you are told,' snapped the girl. 'You don't have to say a word; just take my card to Dr Grunwald without delay.'

The porter was on the point of repeating his objection, but there was such an imperious glint in her eye that he was completely cowed. Maybe he would get the sack for breaking into a meeting of such importance but the girl could not be denied. He showed her to a seat and with a sinking heart took the elevator to the top floor of the building, which was entirely occupied by the executive offices of the directors of the bank and the boardroom where the meeting was in progress. On the way, he idly regarded the card which the girl had given him. Printed on it was the single word, ISIS.

Josef Grunwald looked up with evident irritation. The board were discussing whether the bank should participate in a multi-billion international credit: it was a matter of great importance and there were many technicalities to be considered.

'What do you mean by coming in here without being summoned?' he thundered at the miserable porter who placed the card on the table in front of him.

The outraged director glanced at the slip of card and a remarkable change came over his features. His face went pale and he gasped as if he had been confronted by a dagger rather than a scrap of paper.

'Take the lady to my office and tell her that I shall join her immediately,' he called to the porter, who was slinking out of the room. Turning to his colleagues, he stammered, 'Forgive me, gentlemen, but something of vital importance has turned up. I shall have to leave you to continue the discussion of the credit without me.'

'But Josef,' cried the astonished president of the bank, 'nothing can be more pressing than the matter under discussion. Surely your visitor can wait?'

But Grunwald was already at the door. 'Suspend the meeting for half an hour, or let me know what you decide,' he replied, and slammed the door behind him.

For Josef Grunwald remembered his first encounter with the woman who called herself Isis and who claimed to be both the priestess of the sect and the actual embodiment of the goddess. It had been in a cave, a sort of natural temple on the island of Bali, that he had witnessed the awesome power of Isis to subjugate men and women by arousing their deepest erotic yearnings. Josef Grunwald, financial despot before whom president and tycoons cringed, had become a mere submissive slave to Isis. Whatever she commanded, he had to do, regardless of the consequences. So he hurried into his office to await the woman who had utterly dominated him.

A few minutes later, the door was thrust open and the girl strode into the room. Josef Grunwald gazed at her, amazed and uncomprehending. The person who regarded him with haughty amusement was not the woman he knew as Isis, but somebody he had never seen before in his life.

'What is the meaning of this?' Grunwald spluttered. 'How dare you carry out this impersonation – '

The girl cut him short with a gesture that a stern teacher might use to silence a truculent child. 'Be quiet! There is no impersonation. I have succeeded the person you called Isis and all the power which she held over you and over her other servants is now mine. There is work for you to do. I am Isis and you will obey me: do you understand?'

'What happened to her, the other one?' Grunwald asked in alarm.

'That is no concern of yours,' retorted the new Isis. 'She is a creature of your past: you will never see her again.'

The banker shook his head in bewilderment.

'I see that you are not yet convinced,' his visitor commented drily. 'Perhaps a brief demonstration will remind you of your subjection. Do you remember this?'

She took from the shoulder bag which she was carrying a small box of faded cedar wood and from it she unfolded a scroll of papyrus, brown with the age of centuries. Grunwald watched, wide-eyed. In the cave at Bali, the priestess of Isis had read an incantation which had somehow aroused in him and two companions erotic hallucinations from the influence of which he had never recovered.

'Yes, it is the same one,' the girl told him with a grim smile. In a low, sensual voice she began to chant, apparently reading from the scroll. The words of some strange, ancient language and although Grunwald did not understand them, they seemed to bore into his brain and he was unable to shut them out. For one fleeting moment he had the idea of jumping to his feet and running out of the room to escape from the spell which was being insinuated into his mind, but he was too late and he realized that he was unable to stir from his seat. Then came the images, flickering before his eyes as if he were in the grip of a nightmare.

The familiar furnishings of his office glimmered away and he knew that he was once more back in that rock temple. He could sense the ice-cold walls and the low roof which threatened to press down and crush him. He felt feverish and to add to his discomfort, he was growing a hard-on of such dimensions that he had to unzip his pants to relieve the agony. His fingers worked without the intervention of his brain, as though they had a will of their own or were obedient to the commands of somebody or something outside himself. And before him was the sublime image of the girl whom he was now compelled to accept as Isis. He was unable to say a word, yet she must have known what was passing through his brain for he understood that she disdainfully acknowledged his silent homage.

Josef Grunwald had the eerie experience of watching himself as if he were the sole viewer in a supernatural cinema, and at the same time was appearing on the screen. What he saw was that other Josef Grunwald, grovelling naked at the feet of this miraculous reincarnation of Isis. She was no longer merely a pretty girl dressed in black leather, but a radiant goddess whose clothes were a shimmering sheath of scarlet and gold. He was being torn apart by the frenzy of his desire for her, but Isis regarded him with the same indifference she might show to a worm, yet her very coldness drove him to even wilder excesses of passionate adoration. And the Josef Grunwald who was sitting motionless in his chair, watching his other self, experienced the same pangs of unfulfilled lust, the same overwhelming craving to abase himself before her. And still in his seat, by some magic he could feel the satin smoothness of her skin beneath his fingers and against his lips, while his nostrils avidly drank in her odour, honeyed yet raunchy, which proclaimed her triumphant sexuality. Fascinated, he watched himself licking her shoes and masturbating, and at the same time he felt his own monstrous erection grow until it seemed to draw into itself every cell of his body, and the whole purpose of that body was to serve the superb woman-goddess.

Isis never moved her lips, yet he heard her words reverberating within his skull: 'You are my slave. You belong to Isis, body and soul. You will live for me alone, and if I order it, you will die for me.'

'Yes, yes,' sobbed the seated banker. 'You possess me absolutely.'

Isis smiled and nodded. 'That is enough for now.'

Her words brought him sudden relief. The tension had been unbearable and his emotion too intense to last. With his declaration of surrender to her came his climax: he felt himself shaken by repeated spasms while he watched the violent spurts of sperms erupting from the quivering penis of the other Josef Grunwald, lying at the feet of the woman who had so completely vanquished him.

He became aware that the weird incantation had ceased and he was once more conscious of being in his office. The girl was still sitting in front of him, wearing the clothes in which she had entered the bank and that other Josef Grunwald had disappeared. It was as if the whole illusion had never existed outside his imagination apart from two things. On the girl's lap, there rested the cedar casket into which she was replacing the scroll. And he discovered that his fly was open, exposing a podgy, limp penis while his hands were saturated with a thick, warm, clammy substance which was fast drying into a white paste. He was drenched with sweat and he found himself gasping for breath.

'Now let us deal with your tasks.' Isis spoke with the authority of one who knew that she must be obeyed, and Grunwald bowed his head submissively.

'You are aware that the secret cult of the goddess, Isis, has a devoted band of followers who have set themselves up in the African state of Salamba where they hoped to reconstruct the great, golden statue of Osiris, the god who was the husband of Isis. I have decided that this statue is no longer safe in Salamba and it must be taken to a new shrine where it will be protected from its enemies and those of Isis, and where a new temple will be built from which all the people of the world will eventually be brought to worship Isis and Osiris.'

Grunwald looked sceptical but Isis riveted him with a harsh stare.

'Surely you have not already forgotten what you just experienced?' she demanded. 'Don't you understand that men and women can be controlled by mastery over their lust, just as you have been dominated by the power of Isis, working through me? But this magic, if you like to call it that, is only a feeble shadow of what will be discharged into the world once all the parts of the statue of Osiris have been brought together, especially the Phallus, the one piece which is still outside my grasp. And you, my slave, are going to assist in the recovery of that Phallus as well as with the smuggling of the statue out of Salamba.'

'But where do you intend to build this new shrine, your grand temple?' asked Grunwald.

'Why, here, of course,' replied Isis.

Grunwald goggled in disbelief. 'A shrine to the ancient gods of Egypt in Zurich? Surely you are joking!'

'Do you think that I would have come here and demonstrated my powers to you as a joke?' Isis asked icily. 'No, Zurich is to be the home of the god, Osiris, and of his consort, Isis. I have decided.'

Grunwald shook his head as if to clear his befuddled brain. 'Did you have some precise location in mind?' he asked.

'Naturally. The shrine will be in the vaults beneath this bank.'

'What?' Grunwald shrieked. 'But surely you must see that is impossible.'

'Control men's lust and nothing is impossible,' snapped Isis. 'You cannot resist me, and I shall deal with the other members of your board of directors as I have dealt with you. They will be subjugated and your first task is to set up appointments for me under any pretext you care to invent. Leave the rest to me: I assure you that there will be no opposition to my will.'

'But why here?'

'This is the richest and most influential bank in Switzerland, isn't it?'

'Perhaps in the world,' boasted Grunwald.

'Very well. Once the statue of Osiris is complete, I shall have the emotions of people under my control through their irresistible sexual urges. In addition to that, by placing the shrine here and bringing your colleagues as well as yourself under my sway, I shall have also something else which is brought by vast wealth. And that, my devoted servant, is power. This combination of lust and money will bestow absolute power: the whole world will be subjugated to the cult of Isis, and to me as the living presence of the goddess. As for you, do you dare to defy me?'

Grunwald slumped back in his seat. 'I shall do whatever you command me,' he assented in a hushed, feeble voice. 'My will is your will.'

'So be it,' answered Isis. 'Remember,' she continued in a softer tone, 'my plans seem fantastic to you only because you are accustomed to thinking and working in what you consider a reasonable way. But I bring a new force, the power of the old religion and its magic. Once the universal lust of the people of the world is harnessed, everything becomes possible. You grope through life like a blind man: I bring you light. Believe me, a new age is dawning, the age of Isis, and you have the honour to be among the first servants of the dark goddess. Think of life in the future as being one perpetual orgy into which I can thrust any man or woman whenever I wish.'

Grunwald's head was swimming from his emotional

experience and her heady eloquence. 'Very well. If you have decided that this is to be the site of the temple, it must be so. But I would never have considered Zurich as the carnal capital of mankind.'

'That is because you do not have the imagination to dream of the invincible power which will flow from the fusion of wealth with lust,' retorted Isis.

'What do you want me to do?'

'We shall make our plans for the recovery of the statue and the Golden Phallus, but first of all, it will be necessary for me to interview the other members of your bank's board of directors. See to it. However, perhaps before returning to meet your colleagues, you ought to wash your hands and do up your fly?' suggested the omnipotent priestess.

# 3

## *The Bitch is Switched*

A few weeks before the bizarre seduction of Josef Grunwald, a privately-hired jet swooped in to land at Rome's Leonardo da Vinci airport. A white ambulance rushed along the runway to meet the plane, its siren howling and headlights flashing. A mobile staircase was swiftly moved into place, the cabin door thrown open and three passengers hurried out of the plane and into the waiting ambulance. One of them was a distinguished-looking man in his mid-fifties with iron grey hair, wearing the heavy tortoise-shell glasses and sober, formal suit favoured by world-famous surgeons. Beside him was a young woman dressed in a dazzling white linen nurse's uniform. The third person was barely visible, a supine figure huddled beneath blankets on a stretcher carried by two men from the ambulance. Once the party was inside, the ambulance tore away.

When it was clear of the approach road to the airport, the ambulance continued at a more leisurely pace. It left the autostrada well before the city centre and followed a quiet road through a sleepy suburb until it stopped before a barred iron gate, set in a high stone wall. From a small lodge guarding the entrance, a burly man emerged and opened the gate. At the end of a drive, there stood a low rambling building of crumbling stone, quite hidden from the road by the wall and the trees and bushes which flanked the drive. A wooden sign proclaimed that this was St George's Sanatorium and, in smaller print, that it was supported entirely by voluntary contributions and catered for the health of the expatriate English and Scottish residents of the Eternal City. The paint was flaking off the notice board and the place had an air of desolation which suggested that either the British population of Rome enjoyed such robust health that the sanatorium was no longer required or that they now gave their patronage to more modern and more convenient establishments.

Not that St George's Sanatorium was completely deserted. Two attendants escorted the trio from the ambulance into the building, but they gave the impression that they might be prison warders or security guards rather than members of a nursing staff.

The patient was carried into a high-ceilinged room and dumped unceremoniously on to an old-fashioned iron bedstead. The body was that of a young woman, her features were deathly white and it was impossible to judge whether she was alive or dead. The doctor gave her a cursory examination and the nurse threw a dirty, thread-bare blanket over her. Then they left the room and one of the attendants locked the door behind them.

At the end of a corridor was a room in which a table had been laid and the two travellers were served with a simple meal of soup and pasta and then were shown into adjacent bedrooms which had been prepared for them. In his room the doctor took a number of packets and bottles of medicaments, hypodermic syringes and other items of professional paraphernalia from a case which he had brought with him, and arranged them on a couple of dusty shelves. In the next room the girl dressed as a nurse also unpacked a case, but her luggage consisted almost entirely of clothes which had been styled with that combination of sexiness and high fashion which costs a great deal of money. There was also a strange casket of cedar wood which the girl fingered curiously until she discovered a hidden spring which opened the box. From it, she drew a piece of papyrus, rolled into a scroll, and a number of other scraps of paper which she studied carefully. It was evening before the two of them met again and went back to the room where they had left their insensible companion.

Some colour had returned to the woman's cheeks but she had not stirred since she had been thrown on to the bed. The man frowned, took her wrist and felt her pulse.

'Is she all right?' asked the nurse.

By way of answer, the doctor slapped the unconscious woman's face hard. She moaned and shook her head. He hit her again twice and her eyes flickered open. She stared at the unfamiliar room in alarm, then rubbed her bruised cheek.

'Where am I?' she mumbled. 'Andrew, is that you?'

'Of course it is,' the doctor replied abruptly. 'Come on, pull yourself together, woman. Don't you remember, we were in Paris, trying to grab the Golden Phallus?'

'The Phallus, yes, of course. Where is it?'

'You are still confused. That Professor Halevy has it: we had to get the hell out of the place when that big black man got his head blown off and there were police all over the place.'

Recollection flooded back and the woman tried to raise herself from the bed, but Andrew Drummond pushed her back.

'Relax, Isis,' he said with a humourless smile. 'You aren't going anywhere.'

'We have to get the Golden Phallus,' Isis answered impatiently. 'Where am I?' She pointed at the girl. 'Who is this woman?'

The girl grinned down at her. 'My name is Anna, but it will be Isis.'

Again Isis attempted to rise but Drummond roughly thrust her back against the mattress.

'Anna was with Asi Moriba, the guy who was shot, but

now she has teamed up with me,' he told her. 'You see, although, like us, she failed to steal the Golden Phallus, she and Moriba had taken the head of the statue which had turned up in Egypt and I guess that she is the only living person who knows where it is hidden.'

'She must give it to me. I am Isis and the restoration of the golden statue of Osiris has been entrusted to me. Don't forget, Andrew Drummond, that you have taken an oath to serve me. Now, let me get up, at once.'

Anna strode over to the bed, pulled aside the blanket and gripped the prostrate Isis by her arms, pinning her down.

'Listen, sister,' she hissed, 'try and get this into your dumb head. Whatever you might have been once, now you are nothing, nothing at all. Do you understand?'

Hatred burned in Isis's black, almond-shaped eyes, but she quailed before Anna's hard, cold glare.

'Andrew,' she cried, 'take her away!'

But Drummond had produced a hypodermic which he filled from a phial. 'You are overexcited,' he said in a flat, unemotional voice. 'This will quieten you down, and when you are calm, we shall talk.'

Isis tried to struggle, but Anna held her down firmly and her lips curved into a sadistic smile as the needle sank into Isis's arm and Drummond pressed home the plunger. Anna kept grasping her until she felt the fight go out of Isis.

'You are finished,' Anna spoke quietly, but there was a menace in her voice which brought a shiver down the spine of her drugged victim. 'You will reveal to me the mysteries of Isis, and I shall replace you and succeed where you have failed.'

Isis gazed at Andrew Drummond, but now her eyes pleaded piteously where before they had commanded.

He gave her a frosty smile. 'What Anna says is true.

We need to know your secrets, the key to the sexual power of Isis, and you will tell us. Not at once, but we have time, and I have the drugs which will compel you to cooperate. You have driven men crazy with desire. Well, now it is your turn to have a taste of your own medicine. Modern science is not so glamorous as your black magic, but you will see that it is just as effective in a rather nasty way. Now you will rest while that shot works on your brain. You will notice the way it saps your willpower. Tomorrow, we step up the dose. Good night.'

With a brisk nod of his head, he walked out of the room followed by Anna.

'Sweet dreams,' called Anna, as she turned off the light and locked the door behind them.

The next day, they brought her a little food but Isis lacked an appetite and even before her second injection, she was conscious of a weariness in her limbs and her brain seemed to be wrapped in cotton wool. The idea of escaping flitted through her mind but all her instincts warned her that it was impossible and she could not fight against the torpor which crept through her body, as persistent and debilitating as an autumn fog. Neither Andrew Drummond nor Anna said another word to her. When she tried to ask questions, they ignored her, confining their actions to bringing her scanty meals three times a day, always accompanied by whatever it was that was in the syringe, and checking her temperature, pulse and blood pressure.

The treatment continued for a week, but after two or three days the helpless woman lost all track of time. She no longer struggled against the needle and she weakly allowed Anna to feed her since she was either not capable of feeding herself or not sufficiently motivated to eat. And every day the cotton wool grew thicker around her brain, her consciousness seemed to dwindle away and her limbs felt heavier.

Then one morning, the routine changed. She was given her shot but there was something else in the syringe which stung as it coursed into her bloodstream. For a moment her head cleared, only to be followed by a new and alarming sensation as if her brain were on fire. She shook her head petulantly and Anna pulled her up in the bed to a sitting position. Drummond watched her, a sardonic smile playing over his lips. Meanwhile, Anna had retrieved the cedar casket and extracted the scroll and the other pieces of paper.

'Now,' she said in a soft, menacing voice, 'you will explain how you play your tricks as priestess or witch. Tell me how it is done.'

It took all Isis's energy and willpower to shake her head. Anna slapped her face and she slumped back against the pillows.

'Let's try again,' Anna said, but Isis remained silent.

'Strip her and throw her on the floor,' Drummond told Anna.

Isis was wearing only a flimsy hospital gown. Anna tore it off her and hurled the naked woman out of bed and on to the stone floor. Isis was dizzy and it felt as if her head were floating above her, but her arms and legs had been turned to lead. She made no effort to rise but lay still at their feet. Still she would not speak.

'Stubborn little bitch, aren't you?' Drummond commented. 'But it won't do you any good. We shall break you and you will babble out all your secrets.'

They stepped up the treatment and she drifted between spells of coma and being fully awake. She had visions and nightmares and often did not know whether Drummond and Anna were really with her in the room or were memories in her fevered mind. She must have spoken to them, but she had no recollection of uttering a word, yet she distinctly heard her own voice. They pumped drugs into her and drew out her thoughts as if with the same syringe. The casket was brought to her and it loomed up as though it were going to swallow her. In panic, she blurted out how to read the hieroglyphics on the scroll and all the hidden things of necromancy and the bending of minds and wills, the arts of Isis which had been passed on to her by the former priestess and which had been handed down from generation to generation throughout the centuries, ever since Isis and Osiris had been worshipped by all the people of Upper Egypt and many lands beyond. She would tell them anything as long as she was not entombed in the dreadful cedar box. And although she did not see them, her two inquisitors listened carefully to every word and recorded all her delirium so that not a syllable was lost.

Yet they were not satisfied. It was another day and again she was on the ground, naked, her teeth chattering from cold and from fear. Anna stood before her, holding the scroll, aloof and dominant.

'Let's see if you have been telling the truth,' she said, and she began to read from the scroll.

The woman who had been Isis heard the words and shuddered. They sounded her defeat and her abasement. The divinity which had been entrusted to her had become the possession of another and she who had been used to command now would be compelled to obey. Even in her weakened physical state, she could not resist the waves of lust which flooded through her. Anna had learned her lessons thoroughly and she intoned the weird chant exactly as the other woman had unknowingly taught her. Her wretched mentor sobbed at her feet, begging for yet more complete humiliation. Now that her ordeal was at an end, Anna allowed the besotted woman the consolation of kissing and licking her arse and her cunt. Andrew Drummond watched, spellbound, as one woman worshipped the body of the other.

Despite her newly-acquired divinity, Anna found herself getting turned on. In her time, she had made love to many men and women, but she had never experienced such complete adulation. Her victim could deny her nothing and would do anything she ordered, no matter how grotesque or revolting. Her lips and tongue were warm and caressing, so Anna lay back and accepted what the other so willingly offered. As her excitement mounted, she became aware of Andrew Drummond, his cock distended, approaching her and she took him in her mouth while her slave drew her tongue across the full, red cherry of her clitoris.

Such was Anna's triumphant exultation that she came very quickly, brutally pressing down on the servile Isis. She felt Drummond's penis, hard and urgent, between her lips, but she drew her mouth away and pointed at the prostrate priestess.

'Finish yourself off inside her,' she commanded.

Drummond picked her up and went to slide his penis inside her, but the woman screamed and started to struggle.

'Do not dare to defile me! Do you not know that my life and my body were entirely devoted to the goddess?'

'It's true,' gasped Drummond. 'My God, a woman who has spent her life in the service of lust, and she was a virgin until we gave her to that dirty little doctor in Paris as the price of his cooperation in getting us out of the country!'

'Let me be,' shrieked the distraught woman.

'Come now, it's never so bad after the first time. But you should still be nice and tight: this will be an unexpected pleasure,' Drummond gloated.

Still she struggled until Anna rose to her feet and ordered her to submit. At once, she grew passive and meekly accepted the surgeon's strong member with its heavy, blue knotted veins, first in her mouth and then inside her. Anna watched contentedly what was an act of sheer rape, for there was nothing subtle or tender in Drummond's love-making. The woman was for him a mere receptacle into which he drove pitilessly. Her arms and thighs were bruised where he roughly held her down and she whimpered like a whipped dog as again and again he shot his semen inside her, but she did not attempt to resist or to complain. Her mortification was complete and Anna smiled her approval. Dazed and violated, the women was left spread-eagled on the floor. Drummond wiped himself on the gown which had been torn from the broken creature, and he and Anna left the room without casting another glance at her.

Time passed, but the prostrate woman had no notion of whether it was minutes or hours. What eventually aroused her from her trance-like state was the cold which seeped through her bare limbs. She crawled to where her soiled hospital gown had been tossed and struggled to put it on. It was thin and rough against her skin but it was a welcome relief from her nudity. Her befuddled brain could not distinguish between recollections of what had occurred and the hallucinations which had been instilled into her mind by the malignant drugs. She rested herself on the bed and closed her eyes.

In a dull way, she recognized that something real had happened to her. Her body ached as though all her tendons had been stretched on a rack, her skin was so bruised that even the pressure of her fingers on it was agonizing. The trickle of warm, sticky blood between her thighs was no fiction. In a vague way she knew that although her ordeal had ceased, she was still in danger.

She could not conceive what else might happen to her, but her instincts told her that she must get away. It required a superhuman effort to climb off the bed and the floor seemed to sway dizzily, yet somehow she managed to totter to the door and turn the handle. It was unlocked, and she crept out into the long, unlit corridor.

She had no idea where she was but at the back of her mind was the conviction that if she were clear of the building she would meet people and that she possessed a power to make them do whatever she wanted. She would order them to take her to safety and in time the mists which swirled in her mind would disperse. Then she would be able to decide what she would have to do. But first she had to negotiate the corridor which appeared to stretch interminably into the gloom. Her legs were weak but she leaned against the wall as she made her snail's pace progress.

Suddenly there was a staircase on her left and she knew that she had to go downstairs if she were to reach the exit from her prison. She staggered and concentrated with all her might on steadying herself for the descent. Perhaps it was because she was so intent on what lay to her left that she did not see the door on her right open and a thickset man in some sort of uniform emerge. The guard glared at her and then struck her a smashing blow which sent her sprawling down the stairs. The impact of the stone steps on her head stunned her, and she lay on a landing, half-conscious, until the guard seized her by her hair and yanked her to her feet.

Anna and Drummond, well pleased with the results of their day's work, were in the makeshift dining room, relaxing with a drink, when they heard the crash. A minute later, one of the guards knocked on the door and entered the room.

'Prisoner tried to escape,' he reported tersely.

'Stupid bitch!' exclaimed Drummond. 'What have you done with her?'

'Shut her back in her room and locked the door,' the guard replied. 'Worked her over a bit first to teach her a lesson,' he added with a grin.

The guard went out and Drummond regarded Anna quizzically. 'Well, what are we going to do with her?' he demanded. 'You do understand, don't you, that as long as she lives, she is your rival?'

'You're crazy!' Anna retorted. 'She's a nothing, a zero. I have taken everything that fucking cow ever had – all the magic, all the power – so what can she do, especially in her state? She's just a junkie, a mindless zombie!'

'It's not that simple,' Andrew Drummond told her thoughtfully. 'She's pretty souped up now, but in time the effect of the stuff will wear off. It does not permanently soften the brain, and she will come to realize what she has done and, although she has revealed all her secrets to you, she won't have forgotten them herself, so she will be capable of exerting all her old powers. Then you can bet that she will be really sore at you, that is, if she is still around.'

Anna stared at him for a moment. Then she spoke quietly and deliberately. 'So you had better make sure that she is not around, hadn't you?'

'I shall deal with the matter in the morning,' he answered. 'At least we can make sure that she enjoys the experience.'

'And so will you, I am certain,' Anna remarked drily.

'Come and watch,' invited Drummond.

Back in her cell, Isis lay shivering in her bed. The guard who had captured her had not been content with punching her aching body and kicking her breasts and belly; when she had laid there, barely conscious and unable to offer any resistance, he had dropped his pants and raped her.

His nails dug into her flesh, raising ugly red weals and when she shook her head in mute protest, he bit her savagely on the throat. There was a merciful numbness which radiated from her womb and she was hardly aware of the man's climax until he had pulled away, struck her once more and left the room. Then she felt his sperm oozing out of her like some evil discharge from a septic wound. Her torments had exhausted her, but sleep would not come and she waited passively for the morning and whatever it might bring.

Her eyes were wide open when Drummond came in and drew the heavy curtain, letting sunshine stream into the room. He nodded to her almost cordially and took her pulse with all the care and attention he lavished on his rich, aristocratic patients in his exclusive clinic. He touched her bruises with exquisitely delicate fingers and smiled encouragingly.

'You know, considering the treatment you have undergone, you are in very good shape,' he pronounced. 'You must have a remarkably healthy constitution.'

Anna had followed him into the room and looked at him enquiringly, but Drummond summoned one of the guards and ordered him to wash Isis.

'And do it gently, man,' he called. 'I don't want her hurt.'

He strode out of the room, leaving Anna to supervise the patient's ablutions: when he returned he was carrying a beaker which contained a purple liquid.

'No more injections for you,' he smiled. 'Just drink this. It will do you good.'

Isis shook her head. Some sixth sense warned her against the draught. Drummond made disapproving tutting sounds and proffered the glass, but Isis turned away angrily. At a sign from Drummond, one of the guards held her down and Anna pinched her nose until she was forced to open her mouth to gulp for air. In one decisive movement, Drummond tipped the contents of the glass into her mouth and forced her to swallow.

'There now, what was all that fuss about? It does not taste that bad, does it?' he said jovially.

'What was it?' Isis demanded fearfully.

'Something very special,' Anna assured her.

The brew was making her feel agitated and she began to toss about feverishly in the bed. Drummond patted her hand soothingly and then started to take off his clothes. There was a red haze before her eyes and she felt rather than saw him climb into the bed, but she was conscious of Anna, standing nearby and watching what was going on. Her pains miraculously died away and there was a comforting glow in her stomach. At the same time, the sense of unease and anxiety which had oppressed her vanished, to be replaced by a feeling of happiness and well-being. Something was sliding inside her and she came to the conclusion that it must be Drummond's penis, but this no longer troubled her. His mouth was pressing down on hers, his tongue inside her mouth. She could not object; in fact it was rather nice. She wanted to move about to heighten the sensation, but she discovered that her limbs no longer obeyed her, so she was obliged to lie still and let the man do all the work. He was gripping her quite tight, but there was no discomfort and while his invading cock was forcing itself harder and deeper inside her, she just smiled contentedly and a great drowsiness descended on her. She hoped that he would come quickly so that he would leave her in peace and she could settle down to sleep, but there was nothing that she could do to help bring him to his climax.

There was something different now being pressed against her lips. Her brain was tired but she knew that moistness and the odour was familiar. Weakly opening her mouth, she let her tongue play against Anna's wet cunt. They could do whatever they wanted with her, but let it be over soon, for she had never known such weariness. She thought that one of them was fondling her breasts: her nipples were straining erect and her flesh was deliciously taut, but she was becoming confused. Yet there was a sort of thirst within her vagina which she felt had to be assuaged before she succumbed to the numbness which was gradually overcoming her weakening senses. Far away she heard a voice, was it Drummond's or was it an echo in her own head?

'Can you think of a better way to go?'

The tinkling laughter which greeted these words must have come from Anna. She wanted to tell them to hurry, but the words would not form in her throat. Just lie back, she told herself, and they would soon go away. It must be evening because it was getting very dark, or was that due to the unbearable weight of her eyelids?

From miles away, she heard Drummond's cry of triumph and fulfilment and something was happening inside her. At the same time, there was a wonderful quaking of the walls of her vagina, something she could not control and which she did not understand. In all her life, she had never experienced anything like it. Her whole body was shaking, but it was perfect bliss. Then she was alone. The night seemed to close in around her, enfolding her in a loving embrace of velvety blackness, and she was free to surrender to the waves of sleep which were overwhelming her.

Drummond and Anna stood together in the bright sunlight. The man pulled on his clothes while Anna looked with cynical amusement at the contented smile on the lips of the dead priestess.

# 4
## *Mr Fixit*

The ACE Office Cleaning and Decontamination Company occupied dingy premises in one of those grey, industrial suburbs of Zurich which are never seen by tourists or those who have business in the financial district of the city. It presented an unwashed window to passing pedestrians, behind which there were displayed four photographs of large factory buildings which presumably had been cleaned or decontaminated by ACE at some time or other, but one could be forgiven for wondering why the company did not set to work cleaning up its own offices. A potential client who was not sufficiently deterred by the unappealing exterior of the place would have found little to encourage him if he ventured within. The plain wooden counter separated him from ceiling-high metal racks on which were arrayed rows of brown cardboard folders, a set of telephone directories which long ago should have been replaced by later editions, and a calendar, also out of date, on which was depicted a faded scene of Mont Blanc peering coyly above a field of edelweiss. A clumsy manual typewriter stood unattended on a table and a typist's chair with a broken back completed the decor. It did not appear a location likely to attract one of Switzerland's leading bankers, yet Josef Grunwald nervously pushed the door open and went inside, after first looking anxiously around him as if to ensure that nobody witnessed him entering such a rundown establishment. He had no need to worry: the shabby side street was quite deserted.

An antique bell clanged, warning anybody in an inner

office that they were no longer alone, and a sandy-haired youth, wearing the sort of brown overall favoured by grocers many years ago, came through a battered wooden door from which the dark varnish was flaking off. He blinked wearily, yawned and asked the newcomer what he wanted.

'I have an appointment with Ben,' Grunwald told him.

'Have you, now,' mused the young man.

Grunwald handed him a visiting card which he examined carefully. The name on it was not that of the banker and there were several barely distinguishable marks like scratches on the reverse. The representative of the ACE Office Cleaning and Decontamination Company nodded and pressed a hidden button. Part of the counter swung aside and Grunwald walked through to the back of the office. He waited until the door in the wall was opened. Passing through it, Grunwald saw that the tatty wooden appearance disguised a robust steel structure such as guarded the vaults in his own bank.

He was in a tiny compartment, not much more than a cubbyhole, which housed a sophisticated miniaturized switchboard which Grunwald imagined was manned by the sandy-haired man who had followed him inside and who signalled to him to climb an open-tread staircase projecting from one of the walls. At the top was yet another door which opened at Grunwald's approach. The banker walked through to the room beyond.

A heavy-jowled man in his thirties was seated behind a desk which, like the rest of the furniture in the room, was considerably more respectable than that which graced the outer offices. Grunwald settled in a deep leather chair while his host turned to a walnut panelled cocktail cabinet and produced bottles, glasses and an ice bucket.

'Let me see,' he said reflectively. 'It's Russian vodka, preferably Stolichnaya, with fresh lime juice, isn't it?'

Grunwald nodded but Ben had already started to pour the drink: he took a straight malt whisky for himself, sat back in his chair and regarded the banker attentively.

'Something has turned up which I would like you to tackle for us,' Grunwald said.

'You know the way I operate. You give me an outline of the job. I assess what would be involved and let you know whether or not I am prepared to do it, and if so how much it is going to cost.'

Grunwald had no illusions on the last point. Ben the Bear was expensive but as effective as a nuclear explosion and just about as ruthless. Grunwald had first come across him when the bank had been faced with what could have been a devastating crisis. A French diplomat had opened a numbered account which was used as a slush fund from which payments were made to some rather shadowy figures in the Middle East and mysteriously certain terrorist groups had then released some European and American hostages. The business was absolutely secret in view of its delicacy so the diplomat had been shattered when he received a blackmail demand from someone who threatened to reveal every detail, down to the number of the bank account. He spoke with the directors of the bank since revelation would discredit them also. The diplomat agreed to play for a little time and he brought in Ben the Bear. He explained to Grunwald that Ben was a freelance who had perhaps once been a Mossad agent, perhaps still was, or perhaps never had been, but that he got things done although his methods tended to be unorthodox. This was confirmed when one of the managers of the bank disappeared.

'It had to be somebody with authority inside the bank,' Ben explained, 'to have known the code and the number of the account. Now, if this was a simple case of returning a stolen document, the trouble would end once the paper was back in your hands. But blackmail is different. The menace is what the guy knows, not something we can take back from him, so the solution has to be surgical.'

The manager was never seen again. Grunwald had been impressed and when, a couple of years later, a particularly valuable consignment of jewels vanished into thin air on their way to the bank, on his own initiative he called in Ben the Bear. His colleagues consulted the Zurich police in whom they had unbounded confidence and they were still going through the process of filling in more and more forms when Ben had the Zurich police chief, who had masterminded the theft, arrested by agents of the Federal Police from Berne. This coup had been a great help to Grunwald's career, and he had continued, when the need arose, to call on the services of the ACE Office Cleaning and Decontamination Company.

But Ben the Bear was not a man who could be taken for granted. He would consider every request and sometimes refuse to take on a case. He would never disclose his reasons for declining: Grunwald wondered whether they were moral or ideological or that he considered that the task would require more men or resources than he commanded. Or perhaps it was simply that Ben reckoned the fee he would demand would be too much for the client and by turning him down, Ben was sparing him embarrassment.

'The bank is interested in recovering certain archaeological curios which have fallen into the wrong hands,' Grunwald informed him.

Ben peered at him from beneath his bushy black eyebrows. 'These curios belong to the bank?'

'No, not exactly.' Grunwald squirmed in his seat. 'Let us say that the bank would like to present them to a suitable museum – or some other institution.'

'I see.' Ben nodded gravely. 'The bank is acting purely from charitable motives, yes?'

'You could say that,' Grunwald conceded.

'What strange behaviour for a bank,' Ben commented acidly. 'But if that is your story, do continue.'

Grunwald told him of the existence of the golden statue of Osiris in Salamba.

'I have heard about that,' Ben remarked. 'The head is missing, isn't it?'

'We have located the head,' Grunwald said. 'There is another component which the statue lacks.'

Ben stared at him, but the banker suddenly felt awkward and reticent.

'It is a male statue,' he explained.

Ben roared with laughter. 'You mean that somewhere there is a great, big, golden prick and you want to get your hands on it?'

Grunwald blushed scarlet and said nothing.

'Come now, don't be shy. Do you have no idea where this sensational object is?'

'It was in Paris and may still be there,' replied Grunwald. 'We do know the identity of a Professor of Egyptology who was in possession of it and who almost certainly would know where it is now.'

'Well, that's a start. So, to sum up, you would like me to snatch a golden statue and spirit it out of Africa and then find the missing bit for you. Is that it?'

Grunwald nodded. 'I'll see what is involved and let you know. Would it be convenient if I called on you at home rather than in your too public office, say in a couple of days' time? How about Thursday evening at ten?'

'That will be fine. I shall make sure that we are not disturbed.'

Ben smiled assent. Grunwald rose and the sandy-haired

young man appeared as if by magic and escorted him off the premises.

At about the same time that this interview was taking place, Cleo Janis was arriving at Zurich's Kloten airport. She had flown out of Ibari, the capital of Salamba, to London, where she had taken a connecting Swissair flight. Cleo was an energetic, bouncy blonde who had a thriving business, managing a string of outrageous pop singers and groups from her giddy glass and chromium eyrie at the summit of a Los Angeles skyscraper. But her life had been changed on that day when she had accompanied Andrew Drummond and Josef Grunwald into the cave at Bali where she had encountered the woman who had been the incarnation of the goddess, Isis. Like the other two, she had fallen under the sexual domination of Isis and she had sworn to serve her with unquestioning obedience. That was the reason she had gone to Salamba and had stayed there until she received a summons from Isis to meet her in Switzerland.

Cleo took a taxi to the Zurich Hotel, a tower which reared up high above the lake and the busy streets. On the twenty-fourth floor she entered the penthouse suite occupied by Isis, and stared perplexedly at the unknown woman lounging on a divan who subjected her to a cold, careful examination.

'There must be a mistake,' Cleo apologized, and turned to leave the room.

'Sit down,' Anna ordered. 'I ordered you to come: you see, I am now Isis.' She pointed to the cedar casket standing on a side table, as if in corroboration.

'The former priestess had to be replaced,' Isis said by way of explanation. 'She attempted to get possession of the Golden Phallus, but she failed. I shall succeed and you will help in the task of restoring the statue and installing it in a suitable temple. You understand that I demand your complete loyalty.'

'Say, sister, how comes that you have the job?' Cleo protested. 'Was there some kind of election and if so, why didn't I hear anything about any change? For all I know you stole that box: your having it proves nothing.'

'I succeeded because I was the chosen one,' Isis retorted. 'You were merely a slave of Isis, and since when did slaves have votes? You are still a slave, my slave, so you will obey. And you cannot think that I stole this from that wretched woman.'

She rose from the divan and crossed the room. Opening a cupboard, she pulled aside a velvet curtain. Cleo looked on curiously and then cried out in astonishment. Displayed before her eyes was a huge sculpted head. It glowed, and she knew that it was solid gold. But the wonder of the object was in the arrogant beauty of the statue's features; the hard, staring eyes, unsmiling lips, finely-chiselled sensitive nose and strong, smooth chin. Cleo had never seen it before but she knew at once that she was in the presence of the missing head of the golden statue of the great god, Osiris.

'Gee whiz, that is utterly fantastic!' Cleo breathed. 'If only it were joined to the body in Salamba.'

'But it will be joined to that body,' Isis agreed, 'only not in Salamba. We are not going to take the head to the body. You are going to help in bringing the body to the head, right here in Zurich.'

'You can't be serious! That thing is guarded day and night by squads of those soldiers, armed to their big white teeth, and with itchy trigger fingers.'

'Don't worry, Cleo. There will be other people to deal with the guards. Your job will be looking after the president. I want Milos distracted so that he does not interfere with the snatch. He will be too busy with your snatch.'

Cleo smiled. She had always rather fancied Milos but had never been in a position to try to realize her erotic fantasies. She looked again at the woman who claimed to have inherited the supernatural powers of ancient Egypt. There was certainly some aura about her, and she was unbelievably attractive. But Cleo herself was a domina ting personality and she saw no reason to weakly acknowledge herself as the other's subject.

'Shall we talk about this?' she suggested.

'We can do more than talk,' Isis smiled. 'First, I have a little present for you.' From the cedar casket, she took out a tiny sachet. 'This perfume is something special. I have kept it for you.'

'Thanks. I'll try it later,' Cleo said.

'No time like the present,' Isis replied, and pulling out the stopper, dabbed a tiny drop of the perfume behind Cleo's ears.

The aroma tickled her nostrils and it had a strange sweetness mingled with something strong and spicy. Cleo knew that this was the personal smell of the other woman, an odour as distinctively her own as her fingerprints or her handwriting. And she knew also that she had to taste what she smelt: the craving was unbearable.

'Come along, Cleo, let's get acquainted.'

Isis took her by the hand and led her into the bedroom. Her fingers moved deftly and she removed Cleo's clothes until the unresisting woman stood before her, absolutely nude and looking pathetically vulnerable. Isis took in the heavy, rounded breasts and the ample swelling of belly and hips with the approving glance of one inspecting her own property. Then she firmly pushed her down on to the enormous bed. The sheets were of black satin which gave an erotic emphasis to the creamy whiteness of Cleo's flesh. Isis had paused to remove her panties but she kept on a bra which was a mere sliver of nylon. Yet, scanty as the garment was, it was a symbol of her mastery over the naked woman beneath her whom lust was driving out of her senses. Cleo gazed up at the irresistible fleshy lips and beckoning clitoris in helpless adoration. Then came the sheer wonder of the feel of them on her lips and around her tongue and she revelled in the taste and scent of the cream which Isis allowed her to drink from her cunt and which she gratefully rubbed all over her face and in her hair. Her idol lowered herself on to the bed and Cleo felt Isis's fingers entering into her own vagina and she knew that she was lubricating as if she had a fountain within her.

She had never known such tenderness and when Isis actually pressed her lips against her clitoris, she could not hold back and came in one glorious orgasm. Isis had not finished with her, and while her body was still throbbing uncontrollably, she was made to go on working with her tongue against the other woman until she too had been brought to her climax. Cleo knew that she had to serve that divine body with everything she had and in any way which Isis demanded and she found this subjection so exciting that she came twice more before Isis thrust her away.

'We mustn't wear you out,' she murmured. 'We have to leave something for Milos, don't we?'

Regretfully, Cleo withdrew. Her body was glowing, but only when she had cooled down somewhat did she become aware of how exhausted she was.

'Whatever you say,' she assented. 'I guess that you are the boss.'

'Don't you ever let yourself forget that for a single moment,' Isis warned her.

It could not have been only the perfume which turned

Cleo on, but once Isis had vanquished her she found the mere presence of the other woman made her itch for the touch of her body. So it was that the following day she had begged to be allowed to go to bed with her again so insistently that eventually Isis relented. Josef Grunwald, visiting Isis, knocked on the door of her suite. There was no response, and finding that the door was unlocked, he walked in. The salon was deserted but from the bedroom there issued a sensual symphony of orgasmic moans and shouts. Thoroughly aroused, the banker tiptoed into the adjacent room and goggled at the sight which confronted him. The two women were reclining on the bed; Isis, as on the previous day, was scantily clad and Cleo, who was stark naked, was frantically eating her. Isis lay back, her eyes half-closed, passively accepting the tribute of her slave. The spectacle was enough to bring even the frigid blood of a Swiss banker to the boil and Grunwald suffered an instant erection, his penis rising as fast as a high-speed elevator in a New York skyscraper. He considered that to fail to join the ladies would be antisocial and a breach of etiquette. He struggled out of his trousers and hurled himself at the tantalizingly exposed backside of Cleo.

The unexpected and unsolicited incursion of a man was unwelcome to Cleo who did not want anything to detract from her concentration on Isis and she shook off her unwelcome admirer as if he were a mosquito or some other garden pest. But Grunwald was too aroused to accept the rebuff, so he turned to Isis and presented his straining penis to her mouth. To his delight, she took him between her full, red lips so deep that he thought that she was going to swallow him. Ecstasy turned to agony as Isis viciously bit into his meaty cock. Grunwald screamed and whipped his savaged member away from her mouth.

'You bitch!' he howled. 'You've drawn blood.'

'Never touch me unless I tell you to do so,' she

commanded. 'Now, as a punishment, stand there and masturbate.'

'It's too sore,' complained Grunwald, tears of pain starting to his eyes.

'That's why it is a punishment,' Isis retorted. 'Now, get on with it.'

Reluctantly, he began to finger himself gingerly. The sudden shock had brought on a chronic case of phallic collapse, but he was so excited by the sight of the two women that his wilted cock soon perked up. Although he was horribly sore, he found himself rubbing harder and harder. He was torn by pain but he had to go on until, with a despairing cry, he came, and sank to his knees beside the bed. With the pulsing spasms of his ejaculation, the torture became excruciating and he closed his eyes. When he opened them again, the women had finished their diversion and both were regarding him with undisguised amusement.

'A little suffering is good for you,' Isis informed him. 'We must arrange more physical torments for you. You will learn to welcome them as special treats.'

Grunwald, in spite of himself, felt a tremor of excitement at her words, and he knew that she had discovered a weakness in his personality of which even he had been unaware.

'What did you want, anyway?' Isis asked.

Grunwald described to her what had happened at his meeting with Ben the Bear and told her that Ben would be coming to his house the next evening.

'Would you care to be present?' he asked. 'Mind you, I cannot guarantee that he will agree to do the job and I am sure that if he does, it will cost an immense amount of money.'

Isis curled her lip in displeasure. 'What do you mean, he may not agree! I shall certainly have a look at this superman of yours and if he does not impress me, I shall not employ him. As for the expense, do not let that worry you. Your bank has plenty of money.'

Grunwald rolled his eyes in horror, but Isis continued unabashed. 'On your introduction, I had an interview with the president of your bank. He is a charming man and will grant me anything I ask. I am seeing some of his colleagues later today, and I am confident that they will prove just as sympathetic and cooperative.'

Grunwald nodded. He could readily visualize the portly president being put through his paces, and he shuddered. 'So I shall expect you tomorrow evening. Our guest is due at ten.'

'I shall be there early. I want to be able to see and hear him but I do not want him to be able to see me. Arrange that. I shall probably bring Cleo with me.'

'It will be as you wish,' Grunwald said.

'Now, go away. I have things to discuss with Cleo.'

He paused only to adjust his clothes. As he left the suite, he called ruefully over his shoulder. 'It's still sore.'

'There's worse in store for you,' Isis promised.

The following evening, when Ben the Bear arrived at Grunwald's tastelessly immense mansion, Isis and Cleo had been installed in a sort of mock minstrels' gallery above the cavernous hall in which the banker received clients he wished to impress. The setting was positively mediaeval, and the lighting was so dim that the two women, crouching behind a balustrade, were quite invisible to anybody in the hall below.

Isis was intrigued by the appearance of their visitor. His black crinkly hair was shot with grey and although she would not judge his age to be more than somewhere in the mid-thirties, his forehead was heavily lined as if his cares had been etched into his features. He moved with a kind of ponderous grace and she was sure that he possessed a hidden agility beneath his slow, deliberate movements. He was indeed a bear. Isis glanced at Cleo. The blonde was unconsciously licking her lips: clearly she would not be averse to getting her teeth into a juicy bear steak, but Isis resolved that she would be the first to taste that meat.

Downstairs, the meeting was brisk and business-like. From his own sources, Ben had obtained a detailed report on the situation in Salamba and he told Grunwald that he was prepared to undertake the mission.

'Since your bank intends to donate the statue to a worthy cause, I would not want to hinder an act of unalloyed altruism,' Ben said, and the look he bestowed on the banker underlined his cynicism. 'So, bearing this in mind, my organization will be at your disposal for a purely nominal fee.'

He then went on to name a figure at which Grunwald turned deathly white and had to sit down. However, he had been told by Isis that he should agree to whatever was proposed. Too deflated to speak, he nodded weakly.

'Don't be so petty-minded,' Ben grinned. 'Remember, we have to mount an entire military operation. It will be like snatching hostages out of an enemy country. Now that needs organization, it needs men and a lot of expensive equipment. And President Milos used to be a guerrilla fighter: he is accustomed to surprise raids, he made enough of them himself in his time. We shall have to come up with some idea for keeping him occupied.'

'I may be able to help you there,' Grunwald said, recalling what Isis had told him of Cleo's possible role. 'And what about the missing thing?'

'The unmentionable phallus,' Ben mocked. 'Tell me the identity of the professor in Paris and I shall have him put under surveillance. When we have recovered the statue, we shall deal with that problem, but it is a matter of one job at a time and I shall need every man at my disposal for Salamba. If we grabbed the phallus first and Milos learned of it, he would double the number of men guarding the statue and probably have the damned thing ringed around with an armoured division and a radar screen. So our first objective must be the statue in Ibari.'

Isis nodded. This man knew what he was talking about and she resolved to add the bear to her menagerie. As for the cost, she was confident that the president of Grunwald's bank would find some way of coping with such trifles.

'And which of the great museums of the world is to be favoured with such a magnificent token of your bank's generosity?' Ben asked casually, as he prepared to leave.

Grunwald was flustered, but he quickly recovered.

'Why, the golden statue will go to the National Museum of Egypt in Cairo, of course. We are speaking about a unique monument of the culture of ancient Egypt, so that is the most appropriate place for it, don't you think?'

'I agree absolutely: an excellent idea.' There was a mischievous twinkle in Ben's eyes as he added, 'So the price I have quoted for this smash and grab raid will cover the cost of transporting the object to Cairo. If you and your fellow directors happen to change your minds and want it delivered somewhere else, that will involve an additional surcharge. Good night, Herr Director, don't bother to come to the door; I can see myself out. Your cheque for half of the amount will be taken as confirmation that we have a deal. I don't need to tell you that a lot of preparation will be necessary but we should be ready to act quite soon after the initial payment.'

With a friendly nod, Ben walked out, leaving Grunwald speechless with indignation. He was still seething when Isis and Cleo Janis joined him.

'Your bear seems the right man for the job,' Isis said. 'I congratulate you on your choice.'

'But didn't you hear what the bastard said?' spluttered the outraged banker. 'God knows how much he will screw us for bringing the statue here!'

'Nonsense!' Isis laughed. 'He knew that you were lying to him so he wanted to teach you a lesson. But while I like the look of the bear, I do not know whether he can be trusted completely, so we shall not tell him where the temple of Isis and Osiris will be located. We'll take delivery in Cairo.'

Grunwald stared uncomprehendingly.

'The difficult thing is getting it away from Milos and Salamba,' she explained. 'Once in Egypt, neatly crated up in a container, it should be easy enough to get it shipped out.'

# 5
## *French Kisses*

Asombolo stood in the VIP lounge at the airport in Ibari, anxiously staring at a dot on the horizon. As Chief Minister of Salamba, he had been kept very busy in the absence of the President and it was with mixed feelings of relief and trepidation that he watched the dot grow into a blob, then a tiny insect and finally into the shape of the presidential jet.

It was nearly two months since Milos had left the country, ostensibly to consult a psychiatrist in Vienna who was celebrated both for his professional skill and his complete discretion. Asombolo was the only person in Salamba to know that the President, tormented by an obsession for a young Scottish singer, Sandra Mitchell, had followed her to Paris where she had been in danger both from the Isis sect and from the ex-police chief of Salamba, Asi Moriba. It was Milos who had broken into Halevy's apartment and shot Moriba. The French had hushed up the scandal: they did not consider that presidents of friendly states gunning down their adversaries would enhance the attractions of Paris to tourists, and since Moriba did not rank high on anybody's Christmas card list, Milos had got away with being spirited out of the country and, as far as the officials were concerned, the incident simply had not taken place. Milos's nervous condition was such that he did in fact go to Vienna, where he underwent a brief course of treatment. But in a country such as Salamba, the prolonged absence of the head of state was an invitation for yet another revolution, hence

Asombolo's sense of relief. What was Milos's mental condition after the best efforts of the Viennese doctor? That was the question which had Asombolo biting his nails.

The plane taxied to a halt at the end of a runway well away from the main apron where commercial airliners were landing and taking off. Asombolo, together with only three trusted bodyguards, was waiting in a large black limousine, and the moment that Milos disembarked, he was hustled into the car and driven off at high speed. Asombolo regarded him in silence. Milos was paler and perhaps a trifle thinner than when he had departed but his minister judged that he looked fit and certainly in better shape than he had feared.

For the whole of the drive to the presidential palace, Milos sat without speaking and Asombolo, after a formal greeting, relapsed into silence. He had no wish to discuss affairs of state in front of guards, no matter how trustworthy. Milos went straight to the room which he used as his study and beckoned to Asombolo to follow him. His first act of state was to pour himself a king-sized whisky.

'Well,' demanded Milos, 'what's been going on while I have been away?'

Asombolo eyed Milos's brimming glass with undisguised envy, but the President evidently was not in a generous mood.

'There was an attempt on the life of the American ambassador by some anarchist group and some fascists retaliated by blowing up the villa of the Soviet ambassador's mistress. The Pope dropped in during his whirlwind African tour and blessed everybody in sight for an hour or two. Although we have no coastline, somehow we got involved in a fishery dispute and the Albanians tried to get us expelled from the United Nations. Oh yes, I nearly forgot, we repudiated our overseas debts, so the Americans have threatened to cut off supplies of their soap operas to the national TV chain and the Japanese say that they will stop selling us video recorders. It's been rather quiet, really,' he concluded.

'Was I missed?' asked Milos.

'Not at all,' Asombolo assured him. 'Everybody has been following the opening games in the African section of the World Cup. Salamba managed a draw with Swaziland and you know that when the football season is in full swing, a detail like the disappearance of the president goes unnoticed.'

Milos frowned. Maybe he should have offered Asombolo a whisky. 'And what about that mob in the temple of Isis? Have they been behaving themselves?'

'I have heard no complaints,' Asombolo said scornfully, 'although I have no idea what they are up to these days. Their priestess seems to have vanished.'

Milos smiled grimly. 'I came across the lady during my travels. She tried to double-cross me, so our agreement with the sect is off. But I still think that there is a future in the temple with its golden statue as a draw for tourists, so I intend to nationalize it.'

Asombolo nodded. He had never been one of the enthusiastic devotees of the cult, but if it brought money into the coffers of Salamba he was prepared to be tolerant.

'As a matter of fact,' the minister added, 'one of the Isis people flew in a couple of days ago from Europe and has been pestering me to arrange for her to see you. An American woman called Cleo something or other.'

'Big blonde, rather good-looking?' Milos queried.

'That's the one. She seems very anxious to have a meeting with you.'

'I wonder what she can want? Anyway, I don't mind seeing her; she could be quite amusing. But there's nothing that she can say that will make me change my mind about taking over the temple, and if she and her friends make a fuss they will all be expelled.'

'Do you honestly think that normal people will come to Salamba to see that statue?' Asombolo asked incredulously. 'There are still bits of it missing, aren't there?'

Milos nodded thoughtfully. 'It's got no head. But more important is its sex organ, which has quite a reputation. We ought to get hold of that.'

He pondered for some time and then turned to Asombolo with a broad grin.

'Listen. In Paris there is this Professor Halevy who had the Golden Phallus. He may have given it to somebody else by now, but he is sure to know where it is and to be able to get his hands on it. I want you to go and see him. Be nice to the old boy, flatter him: you are good at that. Tell him that I have fallen out with Isis, which is true enough, and that we are going to seize the temple and everything that is in it. Let him think that we are ready to sell the statue to a museum of his choosing. That way you should be able to find out where he has stowed the Phallus. Once we know that, let's see if we can't devise a plan to snatch the bloody thing.'

'You are serious?'

'Absolutely. I think that you are right about the statue as it is now, but if we had the Phallus, we would have package tours pouring into Ibari. There's nothing like a bit of black magic for drawing crowds.'

'This thing has bad vibes! Why don't we just stick to football?' groaned Asombolo.

'Because the best we can do is to draw with Swaziland,' retorted Milos. 'I shall get a message off to Halevy at once and I shall make it so tempting that he is bound to agree to talk with you.'

While both Isis and Milos were making their own plans for his future, the good professor was blithely getting ready to entertain a much more welcome visitor. Sandra Mitchell had written to Petra, who she'd met when she was in Ibari, telling her that she would be coming to Paris for a few weeks to star in a cabaret in a fashionable spot called L'Etoile de l'Est. She was going to stay in a hotel, but Halevy wrote back, insisting that she be their guest. He assumed that she would be accompanied by Donald McFee, by now a legendary footballer, who was her steady boyfriend, but when her taxi drew up outside the apartment block, Sandra was alone. Petra embraced her, and Halevy got quite a kick out of watching the two girls. Sandra was a petite blonde with the complexion of a rosebud and a figure of such soft, rounded contours that Halevy could imagine that it would melt away at his touch but for the fact that he had found her a robust performer in the sack. Petra, by contrast tall, dark and willowy, looked equally appetizing and he found the tenderness with which they greeted each other a great turn-on.

'I suppose that Donald could not get away. Is he busy kicking a ball about somewhere in freezing Scotland?' Petra asked, when they were seated in the salon.

Sandra hesitated before answering. 'I don't know where he is. I suppose that he is showing off before tens of thousands of wild fans, probably in Glasgow. You see,' she said wryly, 'we aren't together any more.'

'I'm sorry,' said Petra.

'It couldn't have lasted,' Sandra told her. 'We have such different lifestyles. You know that I insist on my freedom but Donald was sold on a one man-one woman relationship.'

'Really?' Halevy remarked. 'You surprise me. When he was here, I got the impression that he was quite a swinger.'

Sandra laughed bitterly. 'A lot of people act differently

abroad from the way they behave at home. That's the way it was with Donald.'

The trouble had come to a head, she told them, over Laurent Joliot, a whizz kid of an impresario, who had signed Sandra up for her engagement in Paris. She admitted that he had engaged her for rather more than a series of cabaret appearances.

She had met Laurent in his suite at the Dorchester, while he was recruiting talent in London. She knew that he was in his early twenties, yet she was taken by surprise by just how young he appeared. He was wearing blue jeans which were so tight that they seemed to have been sprayed on to his long legs, a flowery silk shirt and one delicate earring. His hair was long, well groomed and tied in a pony tail and he had applied just a trace of eye shadow. But what struck her most forcefully was his immense vitality. His eyes darted as if they were transmitting some inner electricity, and he flashed a smile at her which would have thawed an iceberg. He had fine, delicate fingers, and his hands were never at rest. It was impossible not to be affected by the discharge of such abundant energy, and Sandra felt her own pulse racing as words poured from him in a torrent of wild enthusiasm.

There was an instant sympathy between them: it was as though they had known each other for ages and it was the most natural thing in the world that they ended up in bed together. Sandra found his vivacity undiminished and he proved himself to be a more experienced lover than his youthfulness might have suggested. Furthermore he was delightfully extrovert, quite different from the conventional Donald. He had only the faintest trace of body hair, a mere fuzz of light brown which emphasized the boyishness of his lissom body. But from the waist down, he was all man! He was well-endowed, and he knew exactly what to do with the superb equipment with which he had been favoured. His penis was long, though rather slender, but he manoeuvred it as subtly as if it were a rapier, probing into her relentlessly. They had dispensed with the niceties of foreplay: she wanted him there and then, and he knew it and his own lust matched hers. For all his precocious sophistication, there was a wild, feral scent to his body which made both her thirsting mouth and her voracious cunt salivate for him. The touch of his hands was magic and she felt herself open to him as if he were the first man to have clasped her close and possessed her.

They both knew that this was only a passing encounter, one of those adventures which, while perfect and satisfying, is as evanescent as a soap bubble. They were not soul mates or sweethearts, simply two adults who were mature enough to give and take a moment of absolute bliss. Yet, because it had been so right, it made Sandra conscious of how much had gone wrong in her life with Donald. His love-making, technically impeccable, had become a routine and he resented her finding the variety she needed elsewhere.

Donald was, however, sufficiently sensitive to know when she was having an affair, and when she got home from her escapade with Laurent, there was an almighty row.

'He made a great song and dance about the danger of contracting AIDS,' Sandra complained.

'Aren't you scared?' asked Petra.

'Of course,' Sandra answered, 'but I am not going to let fear dictate how I live. I know that there is a chance of my getting run over, but that does not stop me from crossing the road, and I don't let worry over terrorists, bombs and hijacks prevent me from taking a plane. So I am selective: I don't sleep around with anybody and everybody. Anyway, with Donald, I think that it was only an excuse. There was a deep streak of old-fashioned Scottish puritanism in him. I guess he got it from his damned awful mother who was certain that I was a scarlet woman who was leading her innocent son down the path to damnation and eternal hell fire, or some such rubbish. He became so stiff and formal in bed that you would have imagined that fucking was an obligation instead of a pleasure. So it's over, and he can make do with his ten fine, strapping team mates in the dressing room – and perhaps the referee too if he is feeling that horny.'

'Poor Sandra,' Petra commiserated. 'Still, I am sure that it won't take you long to find someone new.'

'But that is just the point,' Sandra objected. 'I don't want another regular guy. Donald was quite enough: he has cured me of any desire to settle down with the man of my heart. Let me have any sort of relationship with whoever pleases me for as long as it works out, but without any serious commitment. Maybe that will change, but I am simply not yet ready for matrimony by any other name.'

'What you need,' Halevy expounded, 'is a good, stiff drink.'

And that ended the discussion.

During the afternoon Sandra rehearsed her act with the pianist who was going to accompany her and in the evening Louis Halevy and Petra went to see her perform. When she had first appeared in public her gimmick was that she used to play a chorus or two of each number on a saxophone but she considered that that would have been too corny in a smart Parisian club, and with her growing reputation, she no longer felt the need for the instrument to boost her self-confidence. Nevertheless, after what she had told them about the breakdown of her love affair, they found a pathos in the way she put over her sad, romantic songs.

She was wearing an emerald green backless gown, and standing diffidently before her audience, her hair glowing in the spotlight, she looked fragile and paradoxically both childlike and sexy at the same time. Her voice was sweet but subdued, and the chatter at the tables gradually died away as she began to get through to her listeners and break down their initial indifference. There was just a hint of a tremor in her voice as she sang about the loneliness of a woman waiting patiently for her man who she knows is not going to show up. At the end of the number, her voice seemed to float away and dwindle into silence. She stood before them, hopeless and resigned. With the swelling volume of applause, the spell was broken: she took several bows, gave them a more light-hearted encore and eventually joined Petra and Louis at their table. An appreciative management sent over a bottle of vintage champagne. The tension which Sandra always felt before and during her act had dissipated, but the dreamy, sentimental mood which her songs had instilled persisted even after they had returned to the apartment.

They took a nightcap: it was late but they were not tired. Rather, there was an expectancy in the air and Louis Halevy was sexually aroused by the presence of the two attractive girls. He was therefore completely taken by surprise when Petra proposed that she and Sandra should sleep together and he was disappointed that he did not receive an invitation to join them in their room for the night.

'It will only be for tonight, darling,' Petra cajoled. 'Can't you see that beneath the bold face she is putting on it, poor Sandra is really upset by this business with Donald? I could hear it in her voice when she was singing and at a time like this a girl gets more comfort from the presence of another woman than any man can give.'

Sandra was out of the room at the time, and Halevy suggested mildly that she should be consulted, but Petra shook her head.

'Believe me, I understand these things. She would feel awful if you made her think that you were being shut out in the cold because of her.'

'But I am being shut out in the cold,' he protested. 'How do you know that Sandra would not prefer a threesome? After all, it is not as though we are strangers.'

'Don't be insensitive, Louis,' Petra scolded. 'It's much too soon for anything like that. Now, be a nice obedient boy and do as you are told. Take your things into the spare room. The bed is aired, and you can do with a good night's rest. Several of your students have been saying how tired you are looking these days.'

Muttering discontentedly to himself, Halevy went out to remove his toilet things from the bathroom which was en suite with the master bedroom.

In his absence, Sandra returned. 'Where's Louis?' she asked.

'He is sleeping in the spare room tonight,' Petra explained. 'The poor guy has been working far too hard and is so exhausted that he has asked if you would mind sharing the bed with me tonight so that he can sleep without being disturbed.'

'Are you sure? I would not want to interfere with your arrangements,' said Sandra.

'You will be doing us a favour,' Petra replied with a smile.

As soon as Louis Halevy walked back into the salon, Petra got to her feet and kissed him lightly on the cheek.

'So let's get off to bed,' she proposed cheerfully. 'I was telling Sandra how tired you are, darling.'

'Am I?' Halevy grunted. 'I hadn't noticed.'

But Petra was already leading Sandra into the big

bedroom. 'Good night, sleep well,' she called, and she shut the door firmly behind them.

As a consolation, Halevy helped himself to a second nightcap and took himself off to his solitary cell in a thoroughly bad temper. He undressed, washed and brushed his teeth. As he left the bathroom, he heard the muffled voices of the two girls. He could not make out the words but the soft moans and excited, tiny screams of Sandra left him in no doubt about what was going on. His resentment at being excluded rose to a new level – and so did his penis. It was too bad: they were having the time of their lives while he was being condemned to a chronic and undeserved case of blue balls. He knew that the only way he could get relief from this painful state was to masturbate. But it seemed a miserable solution to take himself in hand and indulge in empty fantasies when in the next room there were real women – beautiful, sexy, provocative women for whom he lusted – enjoying each other without a thought for him. It was not to be endured. He tiptoed into the corridor and halted for a moment outside the door of the master bedroom. He could hear the heavy breathing and whispered endearments which increased his indignation – and his desire. Softly he turned the handle and crept into the room.

The girls were far too occupied with each other to notice the arrival of the voyeur. Petra's head was buried between Sandra's thighs, her hands firmly clutching her full, rounded buttocks. Their house guest was lying back, her eyes tightly closed, languidly massaging her own nipples. Hypnotized by the erotic spectacle, Halevy began to fondle his straining, neglected cock.

'Lick it gently,' Sandra implored, as she pushed Petra's head upwards until her tongue was pressing against her clitoris. 'That's so good!'

Halevy agreed silently. Sandra was squirming, as if she

were attempting to escape from Petra, but her lover was not to be denied, and with a sigh, Sandra ruffled her hair and gave up the mock struggle. But now Petra swivelled her own body around until her own clitoris was offered to Sandra's eager lips. Halevy grasped himself with brutal roughness and although the friction was making him sore, he stepped up the rhythm of his solo performance until he was stroking his tormented penis in time with the movements of the delectable heads which were bobbing up and down before him.

Sandra was sobbing, her limbs twitching out of her control as she rushed towards her climax. For a moment, she jerked her head away from Petra's rich, luscious flesh.

'Yes, yes, now – don't stop! Please, faster!' she begged. Her voice was husky and she was gasping for breath, but Petra thrust Sandra's head back hard and forced her to resume dealing with Petra's own needs.

Sandra was crying out and her body shaking frantically as she writhed in the grip of her orgasm but Petra had not yet come and she continued to clasp Sandra hard.

'Go on. You have to work for me now,' she ordered, and Sandra was given no respite until her partner was satisfied.

Petra screamed and threw herself back on the bed: Halevy gazed, fascinated, and was convinced that he could see the convulsions of her hot, wet cunt. At the same time, he realized that he was spurting jets of sperm into the room over the carpet and on to the rumpled sheets of the bed. Guiltily, he turned to leave unobserved but his ejaculation led to his being detected.

'Where did this come from?' Petra demanded querulously, as she wiped the thick white stuff from her hair. It had obviously arrived too late to have anything to do with Sandra.

Turning her head, she saw the man of the house

attempting to withdraw as he rammed his wilting and dejected member back inside his dressing-gown.

'You dirty old man!' she shouted at his retreating back. 'You are a sex maniac.'

Halevy thought that this stricture was rather unfair, considering what he had just witnessed, but decided that this was not the time to get involved in an argument. He closed his bedroom door behind him, stretched out in the bed and was asleep in no time at all.

The next morning neither Petra nor Louis referred to what had occurred, but Halevy fancied that his student eyed him with a somewhat resentful expression. Sandra had joined them for breakfast when they were astonished by the arrival of an early-morning visitor. Halevy opened the door and was confronted by a gigantic black man wearing a chocolate-coloured uniform with gold epaulettes and a hat of which an admiral might have been proud. He gazed down at the professor over whom he towered as if he were a member of some lesser form of life.

'Are you Professor Halevy?' he asked incredulously in a rich bass voice.

Halevy confessed that this was the case.

'Professor Louis Halevy?' persisted the giant.

On receiving confirmation of his precise identity, the stranger produced an envelope which he handed to Halevy.

'My instructions were to hand this to you personally. Please sign this acknowledgement of receipt.'

'Who are you and where do you come from?' Halevy demanded.

'I am a confidential courier from President Milos of Salamba,' he announced haughtily. 'You have in your hands a personal communication from the President himself.'

Halevy was not sure whether he was supposed to be overwhelmed by the significance of the event: it was obvious that the messenger regarded his mission as being of apocalyptic importance. He nodded to Halevy, favoured him with a slight bow and then turned on his heel and strode away.

Petra had followed Halevy into the corridor and was in a state of wild curiosity.

'What the hell was all that about?' she cried. 'Open the letter and tell us what it says.'

Halevy regarded her gravely. 'It is probably a highly confidential document, the contents of which I shall not be at liberty to reveal.'

'Bullshit!' responded Petra. 'Stop playing the pompous old fart!'

'That is no way to address the recipient of a personal communication from the President,' taunted Halevy. 'I should be treated with respect.'

He opened the envelope and extracted a sheet of vellum of impressive quality and thickness which he perused. This is what he read.

Professor Halevy.

You are aware that in my country there is a statue of Osiris which, although incomplete in certain respects, is nevertheless an artefact of considerable archaeological interest. It has come to my knowledge that the people who claim ownership of this statue have no legitimate title to it and consequently it is my intention to claim the statue as property of the State.

The statue is undoubtedly valuable and it should be conserved. I am anxious to consult you, as an expert in this field, with a view to disposing of it, by sale or bequest, to the most appropriate organization. It would be improper for me to deal with this matter myself, but I am despatching the Chief Minister of Salamba, Kirame Asombolo, to discuss with you who should be entrusted with the custody of this object and on what conditions the State of Salamba should divest itself of the statue.

On 6 November, Mr Asombolo will be at the Hotel Grimaldi in Monte Carlo where he will await your call. I appreciate that you will not have authority to represent the party who might ultimately acquire the statue, but a preliminary meeting with Mr Asombolo could elucidate any legal complications and other formalities which may arise.

Halevy folded the letter and replaced it in the envelope. 'It seems that Milos wants to consult me about what to do with the statue of Osiris,' he announced. 'Apparently he wants to negotiate through me.'

'That's fantastic,' Petra breathed. 'Are you going to Salamba, then?'

'No, he proposed a first meeting just to sound each other out on neutral ground. In fact, in Monte Carlo in two days' time.'

'I am surprised that he is ready to leave Salamba so soon after his last trip to Europe,' Sandra observed.

Halevy was on the point of explaining that the President would not be at the meeting in person, but before he could speak, Petra intervened.

'But you can't possibly go. You have your lectures to deliver at the university. Besides, Milos is dangerous. He killed a man in this very flat, didn't he?'

Halevy looked at her suspiciously. 'So what do you suggest?'

'Why don't I go in your place? I could hear what sort of deal Milos has in mind and report back to you.'

Petra was bubbling over with enthusiasm which did nothing to set Halevy's mind at rest.

'That does not sound a very good idea to me,' he replied slowly. 'It would mean your missing hearing my lectures instead of my missing giving them.'

'That would not matter. One less student out of a couple of hundred is not the same thing as there being no lecturer. Anyway, I am sure that you would give me personal tuition afterwards to make up for what I missed. I would enjoy that,' she grinned.

Halevy was not appeased. 'You used to be Milos's mistress. Are you so eager to get back to him? And what about the danger? He might shoot you next time instead of me.'

'It was all over between us long ago,' Petra argued. 'Mind you, we were comrades fighting in the jungle for the revolution and it was a terrific time. But I think that he is still quite fond of me, so I would never be in the sort of danger that you would be at a meeting with him.'

'Maybe some other academic ought to go, somebody who has had no contact with Milos?' Sandra ventured.

'No, no, no!' Petra contradicted. 'Nobody understands him the way I do. Do let me go, Louis, please.'

Halevy fought down his rising temper. The little slut, he thought, she only wants to hop into his bed again. But he gave no sign of his annoyance. Instead he threw up his hands in a gesture of good-humoured resignation. 'Very well, if it means so much to you. I shall discuss with you tomorrow exactly what you can or cannot say, although your main task will be to listen and report back to me accurately. At the hotel, you ask for a Mr Asombolo.'

'What?' Petra's face registered bewilderment.

'You don't think that the president of any country would travel under his own name, do you?' sneered Halevy. 'Don't be so naïve: your lover is coming incognito.'

Petra glared at him, but Sandra hastily tried to divert the storm which was threatening.

'Say, cool it, both of you!' she said. 'Where have you hidden the Golden Phallus, Louis? When that thing was around, there were never these heavy scenes. Maybe you ought to keep it in the apartment until after Petra has got back from seeing Milos.'

'It's safe enough,' Halevy told her. 'It is snugly stowed away in a safe deposit box in the deepest vault of my bank here in Paris. And that is where it is going to stay until I can be sure that there are no more fanatic followers of Isis or any other crackpot sect at liberty who would commit murder to get their hands on it.'

'Are you still worried about them?' asked Petra scornfully.

'Of course I am. Remember the couple whose raid here was interrupted by your Milos with his pocket artillery! They were cold-blooded killers, and they escaped. You can be certain that they are out there somewhere, waiting for an opportunity to try again.'

Petra looked thoughtful, as if she were not wholly convinced. 'Well, perhaps I can persuade Milos to look after them,' she said sweetly. 'He is not the sort of guy to be frightened by a bunch of weirdos!'

Halevy's eyes flashed and Sandra hurriedly excused herself, saying that she had to go round to l'Etoile de l'Est to tidy up a few details with her accompanist before the evening performance.

A sort of sullen peace prevailed until Petra's departure for Monte Carlo. She was in high spirits when she left but Halevy watched her go with scarcely disguised displeasure. Although Sandra had no regrets over her session with Petra, she was unhappy at the friction which had arisen between her and Louis Halevy. He went to the cabaret and watched her act but he was moody and ill at ease and they spoke little when he drove her back to the apartment.

As they got out of the car, Halevy peered into the darkness.

'What's the matter, Louis?' Sandra asked.

He shook his head petulantly. 'There was a man on the

other side of the road. I got the feeling that he was watching us.'

'Well, there's nothing unusual in that, is there? A distinguished-looking man taking a young girl home in the early hours of the morning: a lot of people would have a peep.'

Halevy laughed. 'I guess you are right. I am getting too edgy. Come on, let's get inside before I start seeing spies round every corner.'

Ben the Bear's man who had been detailed to keep the professor under observation watched the light go on in the salon window and settled down to wait.

Upstairs, Halevy poured a couple of brandies and handed one to Sandra. 'Do you miss Donald?' he asked morosely.

'No more than you are missing Petra,' she replied. Then she regretted her words. 'Sorry, that was a bitchy thing to say,' she apologized, and patted his hand sympathetically.

He pulled her close to him and kissed her. 'Come to bed,' he entreated. 'I get lonely.'

'I don't like sleeping alone either,' she admitted. 'You get used to having somebody beside you in the bed. When I was a kid, I had a teddy bear, but I guess I need more lively company these nights.'

'I do a good teddy bear impersonation,' he claimed.

Ben's man noted the light going out in the salon and nodded knowingly as the bedroom was illuminated. He would get photographs of the girl with the professor and send them back to Zurich in case she was of some importance.

Their love-making was a kind of bitter-sweet mutual consolation, but Halevy could not resist an inner smile as he wondered momentarily how Petra was enjoying the acquaintance of her unexpected companion. He buried his face in Sandra's soft, warm breast and dismissed Petra from his thoughts.

Of course he was much older than Donald and nowhere near so agile but Sandra found him almost wistfully tender, and he was a kind, considerate lover. They seemed to melt together effortlessly and he sucked at her nipples as though he could draw love and solace from her body. She clung close to him: there was a comforting male fragrance about him. She wondered whether this was the sort of easy familiarity which tempted some girls to go to bed with their fathers. But she had to acknowledge that he was still virile and the feel of his strong, stiff penis made her quiver with pleasure and anticipation. As his powerful piston strokes grew more insistent, she locked her lips against his and he let her tongue take possession of his mouth. She gripped him between her thighs, drawing him deep inside her and gloried in that miraculous moment when she knew that he had lost control and could not hold back for another second but had to give her every particle of his being. The wonder of giving herself utterly to him and at the same time taking him completely was enough to bring her to erupt into an orgasm which left her panting and drained. His own orgasm although it shook him like a whirlwind.

They did not speak, but held each other close right through the night. It was the love which grows out of a profound friendship, so much closer and sweeter than the sudden gusts of passion which they had both experienced with other partners. In the morning they had their coffee and rolls together and as they left, arm in arm, Louis for the Sorbonne and Sandra to do some shopping, Ben the Bear's man got a couple of excellent shots of them.

# 6

## *Bear-Faced Robbery*

The switchboard of the ACE Cleaning and Decontamination Company was frantically busy. Calls were flooding in from the most unlikely parts of the world, a large proportion of them from Salamba and neighbouring countries. In a cellar below the office and store room, a powerful computer was spewing out operational data which was rushed upstairs to where Ben checked progress reports against a large-scale map of Africa. Both he and the sandy-haired assistant were wearing mechanics' overalls.

'Seems that the good professor has got himself a substitute girlfriend. Charlie has sent a picture of her over the fax. Pretty kid! He does rather well for an old-age pensioner.'

'Don't exaggerate,' Ben told him.

He walked over to the facsimile machine and examined the picture of Sandra which had just been transmitted.

'We'll look into that development later,' he announced tersely. 'Everybody is in position so it's time for us to get moving.'

'Jawohl!' exclaimed his companion, and he made a valiant attempt to click his heels in the approved Prussian military manner, but as he was wearing suede boots the effect was reminiscent of a nervous but good-natured clown.

Ben shook his head disapprovingly. 'Your trouble, Max, is you watch too many spy story videos. Because your grandfather had a sauerkraut factory, that does not qualify you as a German war lord.'

'It was great sauerkraut,' Max objected. 'It was supplied to the army.'

'The American army,' Ben reminded him. 'Now move your arse!'

The two men left the building and Max hung a printed notice on the front door which informed the world that the place was closed for annual stocktaking. Not that the office would be deserted. In Ben's absence, there would be a skeleton staff manning the switchboard and keeping the place operating as a communications centre with which the forces in the field would keep in contact.

The previous day, Petra had flown south for her rendezvous in Monte Carlo. She had delayed her departure until the evening and had spent a large part of the afternoon buying some new sexy clothes in a couple of her favourite boutiques. The truth was that, as Halevy had shrewdly surmised, she was looking forward to the prospect of being briefly reunited with Milos. She could not help contrasting the memory of the nights she had spent with him when he was a charismatic 'freedom fighter' in the tropical jungle with the tame, over-civilized life she shared with a refined academic. Louis was nice, she told herself, considerate and understanding, but he simply did not have the fiery energy, the inexhaustible carnal appetite of Milos. She would have agreed with Max that Louis did not do too badly for a man well past the prime of his youth, but he never could achieve that incandescent splendour she had known with her warrior hero. Perhaps the experience seemed more glamorous in retrospect and she was sentimentalizing, but Petra ached to recapture the old thrill and excitement which had been enhanced by the knowledge that when she had made love with Milos they were the hunted as well as the hunters, and that every minute they spent in their rebel camps, they were in mortal danger. Life with Louis lacked colour and their relationship had become a bit stale. Was it simply that she needed a younger man, she asked herself? It was only in the last few weeks that she had felt this restlessness and the tiny pangs of discontent, in fact ever since Halevy had removed the Golden Phallus from the apartment. Did the thing cast some sort of spell over them, or was she letting her imagination run away with her? Either way, getting back with Milos, if only for a day or two, would be like rejuvenation. So it was with a keen sense of anticipation that she entered the lobby of the Hotel Grimaldi.

She walked over to the reception desk and asked for Mr Asombolo.

'Yes, madam,' said the clerk as he dialled the room number, 'what name shall I say?'

Petra was struck by an impulse. Milos was expecting Louis, so why not give him a pleasant surprise when they met?

'Tell Mr Asombolo that Professor Halevy is downstairs.'

The clerk spoke into the phone and then nodded to Petra. 'Please go up, professor. Fifth floor, the Apollo Suite.'

Asombolo opened the door and he and Petra regarded each other in mutual astonishment. The minister was the first to recover.

'Forgive me,' he said apologetically. 'Do come in. I expected you to be a man. You see, I was told that you were Professor Louis Halevy: I presume that the name should have been Louise.'

Petra continued to stare at this tall black apparition. 'And I expected to see President Milos. Where is he?'

'But the President made it clear in his letter to you that he would not be coming and that I was representing him,' protested the man from Salamba, and he added, reasonably enough, 'so, if for some reason you wanted to see

President Milos, why did you ask at the reception for Mr Asombolo?'

'That bloody bastard Louis,' hissed Petra. 'Of all the low-down, rotten tricks to pull!'

Asombolo frowned. 'Am I to understand that you are not Professor Halevy, then?'

'No more than you are President Milos!' snarled Petra. 'But I am his representative, and I have a letter from him which authorizes me to take his place at this meeting, so I guess that I had better come in and explain what has happened.'

Despite her outburst of temper, Petra had struck Asombolo as an attractive and desirable young woman. He particularly admired her choice of clothes, very feminine but most seductive, he judged. So he was not unwilling to lead her into the lounge and offer her a drink, while he prepared to hear what act of providence was responsible for substituting this pretty girl for some boring elderly professor of Egyptology.

For her part, Petra soon got over the initial disappointment of not finding herself in the arms of her well-remembered lover. His surrogate was quite a handsome stud, and she decided that it would be enjoyable to get more closely acquainted.

'What I don't understand,' said Asombolo, a couple of gin and tonics later, 'is why Professor Halevy did not let you know that the President would not be coming.'

'I suppose it slipped his mind,' Petra replied. 'He tends to be rather forgetful: probably something to do with the male menopause,' she added spitefully.

'I am very glad that you could find the time to take his place.'

'And I do hope you are not too annoyed at having to make do with me.'

Petra crossed her legs and stretched them out so as to show them off to the best advantage.

'I find you absolutely charming.' Asombolo spoke with the heartfelt sincerity of an accomplished politician. 'I am sure that we shall get on every bit as well as if the professor were here in person. Better, in fact,' he said, with a hopeful smile.

'Well, shall we get down to business and talk about this extraordinary statue?'

'No hurry,' answered Milos's most trusted lieutenant. 'It is far too late to deal with that tonight. I insist that you allow me to give you dinner. It will be a meal which you will always remember, I do assure you.'

By the time that they had finished dinner, Petra no longer had any lingering regrets about the failure of Milos to materialize at Monte Carlo. Nor did she trouble to consider in what manner Halevy might be entertaining Sandra. As for the Chief Minister of Salamba, he had come to the conclusion that the negotiations over the statue of Osiris were so complex that he would be obliged to prolong his stay for several days during which he intended to establish the sort of close personal contact with Halevy's representative which is the basis of successful and cordial diplomacy. Or to put the matter more crudely, he considered that it would take more than the charm exuded over one dinner, no matter how lavish, to talk Petra into bed.

While Asombolo was dallying, Ben the Bear and his team were swooping on their prey with the speed and determination of hawks paying a social call on a dozy pigeon. A small fleet of vans of the ACE Office Cleaning and Decontamination Company had converged on Ibari, and at midnight they moved in for the kill. An hour earlier, Cleo Janis had opened the back door of the villa, which had been leased by Isis, to a visitor. President Milos was making a strictly unofficial call.

'It's so good to get away from the palace,' he confided. 'There is no such thing as privacy even in my bedroom. At any hour of the day or night, somebody is sure to burst in with a message of vital importance such as an intelligence report that the Mexican army is being mobilized. Of course next day we learn that it is not true, and even if it were, what the hell would it matter in Salamba? I think that it is a conspiracy against me led by the Archbishop of Ibari: he is the mastermind behind a Moral Majority campaign and the impotent old sod would spread the news all over the papers if he could catch me in the sack illicitly.'

'I am glad that you could get away as we arranged,' Cleo gushed. 'And I promise you that there will be nobody to disturb us here. Now, let me fix you a drink while I slip into something comfortable.'

'Shall we go straight into the bedroom?' suggested Milos. 'I can't be away for too long, otherwise I shall be missed when the next crisis blows up.'

'OK,' grinned Cleo. 'We mustn't expose you to the Archbishop's wrath, must we?'

She led the way into her boudoir which she had carefully arranged for his reception and proceeded to expose him for her own inspection. Milos was taken by surprise by the determination with which Cleo seized the initiative, as well as his own private parts, but it was by no means a disagreeable experience. Before he was fully aware of what was going on, all his clothes were off. His hostess, however, was still covered by the loose scarlet satin gown which swirled and ruffled around her. Milos grabbed her and tried to pull off her dress, but she shook her head.

'Not yet,' she murmured. 'There are other games we can play first.'

Milos went to kiss her, but she turned her head away, leaving him puzzled and angry.

'Stop fooling about,' he ordered. 'It's too late for this hard-to-get nonsense.'

'Tell me,' cooed Cleo seductively, 'have you ever been in bondage to a woman?'

'No I haven't, and I don't want to try now,' snapped the President of Salamba.

'Why not? It's fun: you would enjoy it.'

'I'm not kinky. At least, not that way,' he qualified his statement.

'So how do you know if you have never tried?' Cleo retorted. 'I think that you are scared.'

'I've never been frightened by any woman,' boasted Milos.

'Then try it, just to please me. There's only the two of us here, so you don't have to worry about what other people might think. I know you will like it, and I promise that if you don't, we'll stop at once.'

Milos was unconvinced, but he was too conceited to let Cleo retain the impression that he could not handle any sexual situation, so with a conspicuous lack of enthusiasm, he eventually allowed her to lay him on the bed and to fasten his wrists and ankles securely to the frame.

'Now what?' he demanded impatiently.

But despite his show of indifference, he found the sensation of being absolutely in her power piquant and stimulating. She hovered above him, regarding his immense erection triumphantly.

'Now say you don't like it!' she exulted, and she ran her fingers down the length of his shaft provocatively but too lightly to give him any relief.

Milos strained against the cords but he was unable to

move. Helplessly, he watched Cleo shed her panties and slowly and languorously begin to masturbate in front of him, just out of reach of his mouth. He could see the flecks of white, like the foam of the sea, on the deep red of her tender flesh, and involuntarily he licked his lips.

'Wouldn't you like to kiss my cunt?' Cleo teased, and she moved so close that the heavy tang of her juices invaded his nostrils, but he was denied contact with her.

'My, but aren't you excited!' mused his tormentor, as she inspected his rampant penis.

'I must fuck you,' Milos insisted.

Cleo looked down at him and very deliberately shook her head again. 'No. I don't think that you deserve that treat. Not yet.'

'Now!' he shouted.

'Say please,' Cleo coaxed.

Milos paused, then swallowed his pride. 'Please,' he conceded.

Cleo giggled. 'That's better. But you will still have to wait until I am ready. Do you understand?'

Milos was indignant, but he could not deny that he was very turned on. 'Game's over,' he called. 'Untie me and let's fuck.'

'No way,' smiled Cleo. 'You do what I tell you and we fuck when I say: that is, if I decide to let you fuck me at all.'

'But you promised,' Milos reproached her.

'Sure I promised, but now I have changed my mind.'

Milos suffered a moment of panic. Then he told himself that it was all part of the game, wasn't it? Or was it? He no longer felt sure, and the expression on Cleo's face was enigmatic and only heightened his anxiety. The sooner he was out of his restraints the better, he decided, and the only thing to do was to play along with whatever variations Cleo proposed.

She kept coming tantalizingly close to him and then pulling away. He found that his desire was transformed into a mindless frenzy. She was more desirable than ever now that she was unattainable. Then, at the instant that he despaired of being able to touch her, she suddenly lowered her brimming cunt to his lips. He thrust his tongue deep, deep inside her and felt himself ejaculating wildly against her hand.

Still she would not release him and she made him lick his own semen off her fingers. As soon as he had recuperated, she lowered her body on top of him and fucked him feverishly until both of them had come once more. Milos realized that he was shouting at the top of his voice and that his limbs were soaking wet with sweat and their combined love juices. He was too tired for further activity and Cleo was also clearly fully satisfied. The game was over.

'You did enjoy that, go on, admit it,' Cleo urged.

'It was different,' Milos said. 'Now, it must be getting late and I shall have to sneak back into the palace.'

Cleo looked at her watch.

'It's nearly two,' she announced. 'I'm afraid that I have to go out now. My maid comes to the house at eight to make breakfast and clean up. If you ask her politely, I am sure that she will release you. So long, Mr President. Have a good night.'

'Now, wait a minute,' cried Milos, thoroughly alarmed. 'You can't leave me like this. Think of the Archbishop!'

But Cleo had already left the room, and he heard the front door of the villa close behind her.

While Milos had been involved with Cleo, the soldier on sentry duty outside the mock Gothic structure, originally designed as the Anglican cathedral of Ibari and subsequently handed over to the cult of Isis as a temple to house the statue of Osiris, watched the van of the ACE

Office Cleaning and Decontamination Company which drew up outside. A sturdy man in overalls climbed out and approached him.

'Evening, chummie,' beamed the stranger. 'I have a proposition to put to you. You have a choice. Either you take a goodwill offering from me of a hundred American dollars, or I kill you with this knife. Make up your mind.'

The sentry stared at the wicked-looking blade which had appeared as if by magic and was uncomfortably adjacent to his ribs.

'And if you try to call out, that will automatically forfeit your right to choose the money,' added the man from the cleaning company cheerfully.

The sentry considered the matter carefully for nearly two seconds. 'I take the money.'

'And a very wise decision too,' said his benefactor. 'There are a couple of formalities but, believe me, they are for your own good. We don't want you to get into any trouble after we leave.'

He had been joined by two companions and together they handcuffed the sentry and stuck a gag in his mouth. He rolled his eyes in silent protest, but the man with the knife rebuked him.

'You ought to have more faith in your fellow human beings,' he remonstrated in pained tones. 'I am a man of my word.'

He took ten bills, each of ten dollars, held them beneath the soldier's nose and then stuffed them into the man's trouser pocket. It was a pity, he thought, that the notes were counterfeit but he said nothing since he did not want to spoil the sentry's evident pleasure. He patted the suddenly enriched African on the head, wished him a somewhat premature Happy Christmas and sauntered into the temple.

While this sociable encounter was taking place, a further six vans had driven up and their crews dismounted and joined the first couple of men inside the building. In what had once been intended to be the vestry, a temporary guard room had been set up, but a couple of guards were actually posted in front of the shrine containing the golden statue itself. Before they could utter a challenge, Ben called out to them that they had come to collect the statue for cleaning.

'But it is made of gold: it cannot rust and it is not dirty,' answered one of the men.

'Quite right,' Ben agreed, as he hit him over the head.

'I do hate violence,' Max said sadly, as he disposed of the other soldier. 'You know the world would be a far better place without people like us.'

The other members of the ACE Cleaning and Decontamination Company gang had flitted like shadows into the quiet temple. One of them yanked open the door of the vestry and tossed a metal cylinder inside. As soon as it hit the floor, a cloud of gas streamed from it. The members of the guard who had been sitting at a table or lying on their bunks sprang to their feet but were overcome before they could do anything to interfere with the proceedings. The door was shut tightly on them and, although hardly any of the gas leaked out into the nave, the raiders put on gas masks.

'They should sleep peacefully until breakfast time,' Ben commented. 'Now bring in the tackle.'

A statue of solid gold is an enormously heavy object, but from each of the vans men hauled special equipment. One group attached ropes and chains to the arms and legs of Osiris; others assembled a low trolley which had been transported in sections and on to which the statue was delicately lowered. A long tow rope was fastened on to the trolley, and one of the vans winched it and its load clear of the building. The vehicle's tailboard converted into a ramp: the trolley and statue were heaved inside; the cleaners climbed back into the vans and the convoy moved off into the night. The whole operation had taken barely half an hour.

At five in the morning, the detachment of soldiers who were to relieve the old guard arrived. The sergeant in charge was unable to arouse his slumbering comrades, but the handcuffed guard outside the temple gave a necessarily incomplete account of what had occurred. His acceptance of the hundred dollars inexplicably slipped his memory, but he did recall that all the assailants had emerged from vans bearing the insignia of the ACE Cleaning and Decontamination Company. The sergeant, being an observant man, noticed the absence of the golden statue and acted decisively. The President had to be informed, for he was the Commander in Chief of the Armed Forces. The sergeant could not use the phone in the vestry since the room was still full of the choking gas, and he had not been equipped with a gas mask. Consequently, it was some time later that he was able to alert the command post in the palace, after he had found a public phone box and the necessary coins.

'I must speak with the President,' yelled the sergeant.

'Do you know the time?' boomed a voice at the other end of the line. 'The President is asleep.'

'Wake him up!' implored the sergeant. 'There has been a disaster. The Golden Statue has vanished.'

'Have you been drinking?' accused the voice.

At this point the conversation terminated abruptly since the time had run out, and the sergeant could not find another coin. He rushed back to the temple, borrowed some money from the rest of the guards and hared back to the phone. However, during his absence, the voice had been sufficiently alarmed to take action, and the President's valet had been sent into his bedroom to awaken him. On being informed that the President was not in his room and had obviously not slept in his bed that night, the voice knew enough of Milos's habits to have a good idea of what he had been doing, but no clue as to where. It was important not to start a scandal and when the sergeant called back, the voice told him that the matter would be attended to, but that the President could not be disturbed since he was tied up with business.

'ACE Cleaning and Decontamination Company,' the sergeant called out.

'What are you raving about now?' demanded the voice.

'The statue is in a van belonging to the ACE Cleaning and Decontamination Company,' he explained.

'Is it now,' replied the voice. 'Then it should not be too difficult to find it.'

However, things are rarely as simple as they seem. Once the vans were clear of Ibari, they assembled in a derelict factory building. The statue of Osiris was removed and pushed into a huge metal container which was then winched on to a low-loading trailer. This was towed out on to the road by a jumbo-sized lorry and the whole rig bore signs warning traffic that the load was a component of an atomic power station and should be given a wide berth. The cleaning crews changed into military uniforms, the vans which were already a drab olive green were given army insignia and the transfers proclaiming their civilian ownership peeled off. By the time that the Salamban army had been alerted to intercept the ACE Cleaning and Decontamination Company vans, what purported to be a section of an atomic pile together with its military escort was lumbering on its way to the frontier.

It was shortly after eight that morning when a scared and horrified Salamban housemaid discovered the country's president, bound and naked, on her mistress's bed.

To make sure that she did not publicize this revelation, above all to the Archbishop, she was immediately recruited to the Presidential Household with a salary, paid out of the Secret Service Fund, considerably higher than that of the Chief Minister.

In a neighbouring country, not too well disposed towards Salamba, Ben the Bear had set up his base. It was here that the heavy container was transferred to the hold of a cargo plane, and the force dispersed. When the Salamban army had scoured the roads without finding any trace of the ACE Cleaning and Decontamination Company vans, Milos demanded reports of any unusual or suspicious vehicles which had passed over the frontier. He exploded when he learned of the atomic convoy.

'Goddamnit! Didn't they know that there are no atomic power stations in Salamba?'

'The men thought that it might be some top secret weapon which you had ordered for the army,' apologized the voice.

However, Milos did enjoy one moment of revenge. Cleo Janis was apprehended as she tried to get out of the country, disguised as a nun. She was hauled before him, but he found her defiant and unrepentant. He was puzzled as to why she had not made good her escape as soon as she had left him helpless in her bed. She told him proudly that she had spent the time rounding up all the other members of the Isis sect so that they could get away to safety.

'And now they will be assembling in a new temple of Isis, somewhere you cannot interfere with them,' she exulted.

'Quite a lot of people are going to interfere with you,' Milos growled. 'I have decided that you should be given to the Presidential Guard. There are two hundred of them, but they will have to take turns, not more than twenty on any one night.'

'For the sake of Isis, I gladly accept,' she cried.

'They might still be cannibals,' Milos warned.

'Then they ought to be a hell of a lot more virile than you were!' taunted Cleo.

'Get her out of here,' Milos thundered.

When he had calmed down sufficiently, Milos called Asombolo, who had stayed on in Monte Carlo, and told him what had happened.

'I don't know who that bitch, Isis, hired to carry out this raid, but I want to find out. It was a fantastic piece of organization and I could certainly use the guy who was the brains behind it. I am sure that Cleo Janis knows who it was, and I shall get the name out of her somehow before the Presidential Guard screw her into the ground.'

'What was Cleo Janis doing while all this was going on?' asked Asombolo.

'She was just hanging around,' Milos answered vaguely. 'I have arranged for her to be punished for her part in the snatch, but one day I am going to get my hands on Isis. When I have finished with that motherfucker, she will wish that like Osiris she had merely been cut up into small pieces and buried. There is nothing for you to do in Monte Carlo now, so you might as well come home. There is no point in our continuing to go after the Golden Phallus now that we don't have any statue on which to hang it. I am afraid that your journey has been a complete waste of time.'

'I would not say that,' Asombolo replied. 'I have been able to take advantage of the opportunity of the trip to gain experience and to broaden my mind.'

With a complacent smile, he looked down at the bed in which Petra lay naked and sleeping peacefully.

# 7

# *The Silken Chains of Isis*

Josef Grunwald was at home when he received the call from the officer on duty at the ACE Cleaning and Decontamination Company informing him of the success of Ben's mission. The headless statue of Osiris, still nestling in its container, had been unloaded from the transport plane and was being held in a warehouse on the airfield at Cairo. The airbill and other shipping documents which described the contents of the container as being elements for an atomic power station, manufactured in Arizona and exported from a US military airfield, would be handed over to Grunwald or his representative when he came up with the balance of the agreed payment. He immediately phoned Isis, who told him to meet her at the bank.

When he arrived, Grunwald noticed that there were a large number of workmen bustling about the building. He mentioned this to one of the managers who seemed surprised that Grunwald did not know that work was about to start on the modifications to the bank's vaults.

'There was an announcement last week, but perhaps it was when you were away, Herr Director.'

Grunwald recollected that he had been absent for several days, visiting some industrial companies in France and Germany which were important customers of the bank. Presumably a board meeting had taken place at short notice, and he had not yet seen the minutes. Upstairs, in his office, he was about to ask one of his assistants for an explanation but Isis arrived before he had the chance. With the courtesy which he invariably displayed towards clients, even when they were not beautiful women, Herr Director Grunwald ordered coffee to be brought, and apologized for the inconvenience caused by the workmen.

'To tell you the truth,' he confessed, 'I have no idea what they are doing or who authorized the work.'

'Oh, I can tell you that,' replied Isis. 'I had plans drawn up for the new temple under the bank. While you were away they were approved by the board of directors. I had no time to consult you, but there was no need since you would not raise any objection to anything which I proposed.'

'But how did you get the others to agree?' asked the stupefied banker.

Isis laughed. 'There was no difficulty. You knew that I was seeing each of them, after all it was you who provided the introductions. Don't you remember how persuasive I can be? Anyway, the entire board are now all enthusiastic supporters of the cult of Isis and they could not deny me when I demanded the premises for the temple.'

'You mean that they will sign anything you tell them?' gasped Grunwald.

'Of course they will. Just as you will, my faithful Josef.'

She stared at him as if challenging him to dare to oppose her, but he merely shrugged his shoulders and accepted the inevitable without comment.

'The statue is in Cairo,' Grunwald said wearily. 'Now we shall have to negotiate with Ben for him to bring it to Zurich. That will be expensive.'

'Nonsense,' Isis contradicted. 'He is obviously a man who can be useful but could be dangerous and I do not intend him to know the site of the temple. You will go to Egypt, give him the money, which he has certainly earned, and then arrange yourself for the delivery of the container.'

Grunwald looked unhappy and started to make excuses but Isis interrupted him. She had produced a sheet of paper which she handed to him.

'It is so easy that even you can manage it,' she told him scornfully. 'Read that. It is an order for the shipment of a sealed container to Oslo.'

'Oslo?'

'It's not going anywhere near Oslo,' Isis explained. 'That is simply a blind, in case Ben, or anyone else, gets curious and starts making enquiries. There is a freight flight from Cairo to Oslo: the plane stops at Zurich for refuelling. I have already arranged for the container to be removed and spirited out of the airport.'

'But how?'

'How stupid you are! With the entire board of directors of the leading Swiss bank under my control, do you really think that there was any problem in bribing the right man in the Customs Department?'

Grunwald shook his head, like a boxer who had just stopped a hefty punch. 'But, Anna – ' he started.

'How dare you! At all times you will address me as Isis.'

'Pardon me, I got carried away,' Grunwald stammered abjectly.

'Never forget it. Even when you sleep, you are to dream of me as Isis. Now, what were you trying to say?'

'Simply, how do you expect me to persuade the Egyptians that even a Swiss bank can legitimately be importing part of an atomic pile?'

'You don't have to,' Isis told him, with the assumed patience of a guru addressing a village idiot. 'When you get to Cairo, you switch the papers for these new ones. They describe the contents of the container almost accurately as gold bullion, something which your bank is always moving from one country to another. And before you ask another silly question, of course you pay off the Egyptian customs man. One of your colleagues, who seems to have quite a bit of experience of smuggling, has provided me with the name of the guy to contact. He'll play along. You have no notion of how helpful your board of directors can be, given the right incentive. Now, you had better make your travel arrangements.'

'But your temple will not be finished in time,' Grunwald pointed out.

'Don't let that worry you. Temporary fittings are being brought in so that the place will be ready for the statue to be put in place. We shall celebrate its installation with quite a ceremony: you and all your colleagues will be allowed to participate. As for your excellent Ben the Bear, I presume that he will now concentrate his efforts on the recovery of the Golden Phallus.'

'He has already put Professor Halevy under observation,' Grunwald told her. 'You might like to see this copy of a photograph which one of his men took in Paris. Do you happen to know the girl who is with him?'

Isis's eyes hardened as she regarded the picture of Sandra leaving the apartment block with Halevy.

'So that little bitch is back on the scene, is she! Sure, I know her, and I have a score to settle with her from our last meeting in Salamba. Leave the photo with me: I shall prepare something extra special for her. Now, I have a lot to do to make sure that the temple is ready and I must contact the kids who will be arriving from Salamba. You don't have any news of Cleo Janis, do you?'

Grunwald shook his head.

'Never mind. I am sure that she will be having an enjoyable time,' smiled Isis. 'So, Josef, get your arse into Cairo, pay Ben and get that container away from him.'

Grunwald called the office of the ACE Office Cleaning and Decontamination Company to fix a rendezvous and was astonished to find that Ben was already back in Zurich.

'There was no reason for me to stay on in Egypt,' he pointed out. 'The sand inflames my sinuses, the food is abominable, the women worse, and I loath camels. As soon as you have settled your outstanding account, I shall fly into Paris and personally take over the watch on Professor Halevy. Who is this woman who is going around with him: does she just happen to be one of your Isis groupies?'

Grunwald shook his head. 'She is of no interest to us,' he said curtly.

Ben examined the cheque which Grunwald handed him with exaggerated meticulousness.

'It looks genuine,' he pronounced.

'Nobody has ever questioned the authenticity of one of our cheques,' declared the outraged banker.

'Only joking,' grinned Ben, and he gave Grunwald the documents of title to the container.

After Grunwald had left, Ben scrutinized again a copy of the photograph of Halevy and Sandra. He smiled contentedly. 'You never know,' he mused. 'This part of the job may turn out to be quite enjoyable.'

For his part, Louis Halevy was still uneasy. Maybe the man who loitered in the café opposite was not keeping him under observation, but he always seemed to be around whenever the professor was at home. Sandra was conscious of his disquiet and although she made light of her suspicions, secretly she shared his concern. The subject surfaced at breakfast when Halevy suggested to her that as soon as she had completed her engagement at l'Etoile de l'Est, she should return to London without delay.

'Are you tired of me already?' she asked mockingly.

'I find your company delightful,' was the solemn reply.

'But you know that I am worried for you here. These Isis people attempted to grab you once to trade you for the Golden Phallus. They might try again at any moment.'

'But if they are as well organized as you fear, they could just as easily go for me in London as here is Paris,' Sandra objected. 'And, what about you? Aren't you at risk as well?'

Halevy laughed. 'You forget that Petra stays with me and just what a tough cookie she is. She is thoroughly trained in unarmed combat: I couldn't ask for a more efficient bodyguard.'

'Except for the fact that she does not happen to be here,' Sandra retorted acidly. 'Why hasn't she got back from this meeting with Milos, or whoever it was that turned up in Monte Carlo?'

Halevy shook his head. 'She left a message on my answering machine while we were out at dinner, saying that the negotiations had taken an unexpected turn and she would have to stay on for a few more days.'

'Well then, I'll stay on until she gets back,' said Sandra. 'It will be safer for both of us not to be alone, and I know that you don't object to my company at nights.'

Sandra was still keeping him company next morning when Ben the Bear took over the watch on Halevy's apartment.

Grunwald arrived in Cairo, took delivery of the precious container, swapped the shipping documents and, as Isis had predicted, experienced no difficulty in consigning the cargo to Oslo. Shortly after he had got back to Zurich, the statue was safely in a store room in the bank. And all the time, legions of workmen trudged in and out of the basement of the building and laboured in the very bowels of the earth. In a remarkably short time, the makeshift temple had been completed to the satisfaction of Isis.

'How did you manage to get it done so quickly?' asked Andrew Drummond.

He was seated in the salon of Isis's suite in the Hotel Zurich to which he had been summoned.

'I hired the scenery of the second act of *The Magic Flute* from the local opera house,' she replied. 'It is set in a temple devoted to Isis and Osiris so, provided you do not object to cardboard pillars and canvas walls, it passes quite well. It will do for tonight's ceremony: then we shall get down to constructing a permanent shrine.'

'Maybe I ought to turn up in fancy dress,' commented Drummond drily.

'Do as you please, you will be in for a shock when you see some of the other participants and what they will be wearing,' was Isis's tart rejoinder. 'But I particularly want you to be there. I need to choose a volunteer for a little job, and your advice could be helpful.'

Drummond regarded her thoughtfully.

'I am going to catch that gooey-eyed Scottish tart who caused me a lot of trouble in Salamba. She is in Paris with Halevy, and I am sure that she knows where we can lay our hands on the Golden Phallus. But I particularly want to lay my hands on her.' Isis's eyes flashed vengefully.

'What has that to do with me?' Drummond demanded.

'I shall select a man tonight, during our ceremony of inauguration, to grab the girl. I want somebody who is tough and rough and I consider you to be, together with Asi Moriba, the most accomplished sadist I have ever met.'

'And Moriba is dead,' Drummond said.

'Exactly. So I shall value your judgement. Now, we don't have much time before the ritual is due to start. Leave me. I have to change into the robes of the priestess.'

'Your working clothes,' grinned Drummond mischievously, but he hurried out of the room before Isis had the chance to reply.

It was dark when Grunwald presented himself at the counter of the tobacconist round the corner from the bank. No other customer was there. In the palm of his hand he held a strangely-wrought silver medallion which he showed to the heavily-built man behind the counter. The shopkeeper looked carefully at the effigy of Isis engraved on it and then signalled to Grunwald to go through a door at the back of the shop. The banker followed a newly-built passage which, Grunwald realized with shocked horror, burrowed into the premises of the bank. So much for our vaunted security, he thought grimly. However, at the end of the corridor stood another stout door, and he was subjected to close scrutiny before being allowed to pass through.

He found himself in the midst of a bizarre spectacle. This section of the vaults had been excavated into a great hall and two rows of stately columns divided the space, rather like a church, into a nave and two side aisles. Where an altar might have stood, there were a dozen steps, forming a massive podium. And on this platform was displayed the majestic headless statue of Osiris, its golden torso gleaming mysteriously in the invisible light of a battery of lasers. All around were worshippers of Isis, gazing at the setting with curiosity and admiration, and more were arriving all the time by the same route as Grunwald.

'Don't lean against the wall,' Andrew Drummond warned him, 'or you will bring the whole bloody place down on top of us, like some Swiss Samson.'

Grunwald sprang back in alarm.

'It's not really as flimsy as that,' Drummond laughed, 'but the marble paint is still wet.'

There was a sudden hush of expectation, and then Isis

was among them. Nobody saw her actually come in, but the effect of her apparently materializing was electrifying.

'My faithful followers,' she addressed them, 'you have waited long and worked without ever complaining, and now you will begin to enjoy the fruits of your labours. Here we have a sanctuary, safe from those who hate Isis and would once more destroy the Golden Statue. Gaze on this and marvel at it!'

At her words, a curtain at the back of the temple was drawn back to reveal, in all its lambent beauty, the missing head of Osiris. There was a gasp of wonder, then a mighty shout of exultation from the entire congregation. Even the cynical Drummond was impressed by the skill with which Isis had stage-managed the revelation.

'And now, I ask you to take part in an initiation,' intoned Isis. 'Bring forward the postulants.'

From behind the screen which had adorned the Zurich opera house's last production of *The Magic Flute*, a file of elderly men shuffled forward. With a ghastly shock, Josef Grunwald recognized his colleagues of the board of directors of the bank. As if their mere presence had not been enough of a jolt, the fact that they were all in drag upset his sense of propriety. Surely, it was an outrage that the president of the bank, an august personage in his seventies, should parade himself in a pink mini-skirt? But the sober financiers were well and truly under the influence of Isis, and they regarded her with glazed eyes, awaiting to hear her pleasure and to obey her whims.

From a dozen concealed loudspeakers, there blared out the grossly amplified and distorted introduction of a Strauss waltz. The transvestite bankers responded immediately to the music. Each of them selected a male partner, the bigger, bolder and butchier the better, and led him to a clear space at the feet of the statue where they started to dance. As the couples twirled around in each other's arms, the bankers' skirts flying, Drummond dissolved in mirth.

'Did you ever see anything so ridiculous?' he laughed.

But Josef Grunwald was horror-stricken; there was nothing about the scene which appealed to his limited sense of humour. God, if the customers were to see this!

The music grew louder and Grunwald's colleagues were panting from their unwonted exertions, but the onlookers were clapping their hands in time with the music, spurring them on, and Isis nodded approvingly. Grunwald prayed for the waltz to come to an end but the final, rousing coda brought no relief for the bourgeois bacchanals. It was clear that both they and their partners were thoroughly sexually aroused and before the echoes had died away, the 'gentlemen' had ripped off the skirts of the 'ladies', who exposed their bare buttocks without any trace of shame or embarrassment. Josef Grunwald, however, blushed scarlet and averted his eyes from the dreadful sight. After a minute, he ventured to peep at what was going on, and his worst fears were fully justified. The entire board of directors were being violated, standing and facing the cheering spectators, some of whom were joining in a general, spontaneous orgy. Grunwald turned to Andrew Drummond in the hope of hearing some words of comfort, but the eminent doctor was no longer at his side, having been summoned by Isis to join her.

'What do you think of that one?'

Isis pointed to a huge black man in his twenties who was vigorously pumping into the arse of the director responsible for work in Africa. Drummond watched him carefully for a time, then shook his head.

'Physically, he's great, but you need something more than macho-muscles. Look over there; that fellow has a mean streak about him. See the way he is pinching that poor bastard's balls, and there's spite in every thrust.'

Isis frowned, but turned her gaze to the couple indicated by Drummond. There could be no doubt that the director in charge of unconventional business was suffering. He was being raped with calculated venom by a red-headed boy. She had to admit that there was a ruthlessness in the kid's steel-grey eyes and a harshness in the way he grinned every time his victim squirmed in pain, in comparison with which the black guy appeared positively benevolent.

'He's your man,' Drummond pronounced, and Isis nodded agreement.

The merry-making drew to a conclusion and the bank directors, stunned and sore, were left to recover their composure and lost dignity. Grunwald hurried away to avoid their having to confront them. Drummond led the sadistic youngster to Isis.

'I've a task for you which you are going to enjoy,' she told him.

# Part II
# Penetration

# 8
## *Snitched Snatch*

'So what you are telling me is that this extraordinarily active professor of a dead culture lives, as they say, in sin with a dashing brunette who has been absent for a few days, and he is now shacked up with a luscious blonde?'

'That's the way it is, chief,' answered the faithful sentinel.

Ben the Bear gave a deprecating sigh. 'How can we of the younger generation be expected to lead virtuous lives and grow into upright citizens when our elders set us such evil examples? Well, you can get back to Paris base: I shall take over watching this house of shame and remove you from the dangers of temptation.'

'That's all right, I quite enjoy that kind of danger,' rejoined his aide.

'Piss off when you are told,' Ben grinned. 'I am capable of keeping a fatherly eye on both the blonde and the brunette, if she comes back, without any assistance from a pimply adolescent like you.'

'Pimples are a sign of virility,' replied the young man with dignity. 'Anyway, why are you continuing to watch the apartment?'

'It is most likely that this golden prick has been stuffed into a bank,' Ben said. 'In that case, I shall have either to wait for the prof to pull it out for some reason, or think of a pretext to persuade him to withdraw it. But it is just possible that he is idiot enough to keep it in his home. Brilliant intellectuals sometimes do the most stupid things, so it will be sensible for me first to have a look around his love nest. If by any chance it is there, it will save us a hell of a lot of trouble.'

'You surely would not be contemplating breaking and entering the premises of a citizen of the French Republic?' uttered his assistant in shocked tones. 'Why, I am virtually certain that would be illegal: you would be setting a bad example for adolescents.'

'Pimply adolescents,' Ben corrected. 'I'll call every morning to see if there is any news. Come on, you only have to walk round the corner, so I'll buy you a drink before you go. We can keep an eye on the place from the café on the other side of the road.'

Ben was not very hopeful at the prospect of finding the Golden Phallus inside the apartment and he set members of his team to discover which bank branch Halevy normally used, although he fully appreciated that the professor might deliberately have visited a different bank on this occasion.

The disappearance of Ben's regular agent was noted by Halevy with relief. There was no reason for him to view the large, shaggy man who was sipping his coffee and reading *Le Monde* with any misgiving. Ben registered the time of the professor's departure for the university: it tallied with what had been reported to him, so it should not be too difficult to get into the flat when its owner was out. The problem was the girl, since she did not follow a regular routine. While he pondered how to deal with his quandary, Ben became aware that he was not the only person watching the entrance to the apartment block.

Isis had briefed her thug on Sandra and Halevy.

'I want that girl here, and alive,' she told him. 'But I don't care if she gets a bit damaged in the process. You can do what you like with the old guy; he is absolutely expendable, so if he's in your way, deal with him decisively.'

Drummond had judged his man well. Rory Burke had

been a mercenary in Nigeria, where he had killed Biafrans, in Tchad, where he had killed Libyans, and for a brief period with the Contras in Nicaragua. However, some unpleasantness with an American priest and some nuns led to his hurried departure in order to stifle a scandal. He had found his way into the Isis sect through his brother, Sean, a rather more restrained character who used to market funny cigarettes in California until Cleo Janis had gathered him up for the cause. Rory had 'terminated' prisoners with his bare hands and where his brothers and sisters in Isis had visions of sexual fantasies when their priestess officiated, Rory saw himself twisting the guts out of bleeding victims, male and female. He was disappointed that he was not being allowed to assassinate Sandra; taking her prisoner was a more difficult proposition and despite Isis's permissive order, much less fun. It also entailed working with other people.

'He can take her to the Clinique St-André, the hideout in Paris we used before. Dr Gaveau will cooperate,' Drummond told Isis with a sardonic leer. 'If you blackmail a man once, you can always do it again, so he will be nice and docile.'

'I'll need wheels.' Rory growled.

'Borrow an ambulance from the clinic,' Isis replied. 'Who do you want as a driver?'

'I'll take Sean. He's a mad bastard when he gets hold of any sort of motor. He'll have the time of his life with the bell and siren and flashing lights.'

It was agreed that once Sandra was safely inside the clinic, Rory would call Isis, who would be responsible for her travel arrangements and further entertainment. Armed with a letter from Andrew Drummond, the brothers had presented themselves to Dr Gaveau who reluctantly acquiesced in the use of the clinic. But when it came to lending them an ambulance, he flatly refused.

'That would be madness. Don't you know that the name of the clinic is painted on the side of all the ambulances? Do you want to advertise to all the world where you have taken the girl?'

Rory proposed breaking his arms, but Sean pointed out that this would not help them to find a vehicle and it might result in the doctor becoming less helpful. Then he had a flash of inspiration. 'Wouldn't it be possible for us to hire a good, commodious hearse to remove the lady in style? Surely, with all these doctors working away by day and by night, there must be as many hearses as there are ambulances running in and out of the place.'

Gaveau scowled resentfully at the good-natured Irishman, but when he had simmered down he admitted that he had the contacts who would not prove to be inquisitive and who could provide Sean with a dignified vehicle, which had on occasions been used for the transportation of dubious cargoes.

Like Ben, Rory found the irregularity of Sandra's movements during the day annoying. However, her engagement at the cabaret had ended, and she and Halevy would eat out in the evening and return to the flat together, a circumstance which was soon noticed by both watchers.

On the third night after Ben's arrival in Paris, he and Max were in the service flat which had been leased as headquarters for the group. One of his men had just reported that the professor and his girlfriend had left in their car, presumably to have dinner in a restaurant some distance away. Ben picked up the tiny walkie-talkie transceiver.

'Jimmy, is that ugly-looking guy still hanging around?'

'Sure thing, Ben. And the weirdest thing! You know what? A dirty great corpse-wagon has just rolled up and our voyeur chatted with the driver as though they were long lost brothers.'

'Is that so,' Ben answered thoughtfully. 'A hearse. Is it still there?'

'It's parked about a hundred metres up the street.'

'I'll be right over to relieve you,' Ben told him. Turning to Max, he said, 'Stand by here in case I need you.'

Jimmy was sitting in a shabby red Renault almost directly in front of the apartment block. As he passed the stationary hearse, Ben saw that a man was seated inside, looking in the direction of the café where Rory was nursing a large glass of beer. As Ben approached, Jimmy casually got out of the car and sauntered into the nearby café. At the moment that his body obstructed Rory's view of the Renault, Ben slipped into the driving seat.

It was quite late when Sandra and Louis Halevy returned. The café had closed and the street appeared to be deserted but Ben had seen Rory slink into the doorway of the apartment building where he would not be noticed by anyone walking past. Halevy parked the car at the first available space which Ben had contrived should be right in front of the Renault. As he and Sandra got out, Rory emerged and ran towards them. At once, Ben heard the engine of the hearse start, and the heavy vehicle began to trundle up the road.

Everything happened very fast. Halevy looked up warily at the sole man in the street who had come from nowhere, but Rory was on him in a flash and dealt him a murderous blow on the head with a thick metal rod and the professor ceased to take an active interest in the proceedings. Before she could react, Sandra found that Halevy's assailant had gripped her arm and was hustling her towards the approaching hearse.

But Ben was already out of the Renault, and he hurled himself on to Rory. The brothers were taken by surprise by this uninvited participant. Sean, guessing that Rory might appreciate some assistance, jammed on the hearse's brakes, opened the door and leaped into the fray. This proved to be ill advised. Before he could intervene, Ben had seized Rory's right arm, pulled it hard behind his back and by swift and brutal pressure of his foot on Rory's back, broken the arm and sent the metal rod clattering on to the pavement. The Irishman swayed and fell, screaming in agony and it was at this juncture that Sean arrived on the scene, just in time to receive a slashing karate blow to the throat which had a serious effect on his health, and he joined his brother on the ground. Rory was still conscious, but contact with Ben's boot soon rectified this oversight. Ben grinned at Sandra.

'Can you do something to revive Uncle, while I take care of the twins?' he asked.

Sandra had propped up the recumbent Halevy and she cried out to Ben in alarm, 'Is he dead?'

Ben glanced at the stricken academic and shook his head. 'It takes more than a friendly tap on the cranium to kill an intellectual. I reckon that he would appreciate some mouth to mouth resuscitation on your part.' He had whipped out his transceiver and called, 'Max, come!'

Then, replacing his walkie-talkie, he opened the door of the hearse and started to stow the brothers inside. Sean opened one bleary eye as if he were questioning how providence could have become so malign as to introduce Ben into what had been intended to be a private function. But his persecutor cut short such deliberations by a blow which cracked his head against the kerb.

'You know, I believe that you can get fined for leaving litter in the streets,' observed Max, who had practically gone supersonic in response to Ben's summons.

Together they laid the insensible brothers in the back of the hearse.

'Take them somewhere into the country where you won't be disturbed and persuade them to tell you where they have come from and who sent them,' Ben told Max. 'Then call me back, and we shall decide on how to dispose of them.'

'They really look the part,' Max said admiringly. 'Even the cops will take their hats off out of respect as we pass by.'

Max climbed into the driving seat of the hearse, whistled a couple of bars of Chopin's funeral march, and drove off into the night. During the latter part of the operation, Louis Halevy had responded to Sandra'a efforts at first aid, and had recovered consciousness. Ben favoured him with a smile.

'Well now, Uncle, are you feeling better after your nap?'

Halevy fingered the top of his head and winced.

'I suggest that you take him inside,' Ben said to Sandra. 'If he goes on sitting on the pavement, he'll end up with a nasty case of piles.'

'Please come up with us,' Halevy spoke with a muzzy voice and he painfully got to his feet, leaning heavily on Sandra. 'We obviously owe our lives to you, and I would like to find some way of expressing our gratitude.'

'Yes, I could do with a drink,' Ben replied.

He took Halevy's other arm, and the three of them went into the lobby of the block. During the day, there was a concierge on duty, but at night anybody could enter who knew the combination of letters to tap out on the finger pad outside the front door, and Ben watched carefully as Sandra pressed the keys.

Inside the apartment, Sandra got drinks for them while Ben examined Halevy's head.

'You'll have a nasty bruise,' he pronounced, 'but I don't think that it will be more serious than that. If you feel anything worse than a hangover type of headache, get yourself X-rayed.'

Halevy nodded, and groaned when he moved his head. 'Tell me, how did you come to be there and how were you able to act so swiftly? You could only have had a split second's warning that we were being attacked.'

Ben decided to ignore the first question. 'It was not so sudden. You see, I spotted the hearse. Now, what would a hearse be doing on the street after midnight? No self-respecting corpse would be seen out at that hour, and I did not get the impression that it was an undertaker trying to pick up a hooker.'

'But you were not alone,' Sandra said slowly. 'And I saw you call up help on a walkie-talkie. Do you run some sort of security service?'

'You could say that,' Ben answered genially.

'In which case,' Halevy said, 'I have a proposition to put to you. I feel that I can trust you, and you and your organization are obviously efficient. This attack which you foiled is almost sure to be repeated. We need protection and I would like to hire you.'

'I don't come cheap,' warned Ben.

'I am prepared to pay whatever I can afford,' Halevy answered with dignity.

'I can't ask more than that,' Ben conceded. 'It strikes me that it is the lady who was being threatened: you were merely in the way.'

'It is more complicated,' said Halevy, and he explained to Ben the dangers which engulfed them because of their involvement with the Golden Phallus. Ben listened with rapt attention.

At the end of Halevy's recital, he asked. 'This relic, the phallus or whatever it is, can I see it?'

Halevy shook his head. 'I have put it in a safe deposit

box in my bank,' he told Ben. 'It would not have been secure in the flat.'

'Quite right. But why don't you present the thing to some museum and get shot of it?'

'You do not understand. I am making arrangements, but it takes time. You see, this is not any old piece of junk. It is absolutely unique and there are a lot of formalities before I can get permission to export it, and the trustees of the National Museum of Egypt have to meet in Cairo and go through the rigmarole of accepting it. Meanwhile, are you willing to protect it, as well as ourselves?'

'I don't see why not,' smiled Ben. 'We can agree on a reasonable fee. But I will have to see the thing and actually have it in my hands.'

'We can fix a date tomorrow,' Halevy said. 'I can't tell you how glad I am that we have somebody as capable as you to help us.'

Sandra had been looking over this chunky stranger, and she felt glad also that he would be around, but her sentiments were somewhat different from those of their host.

As for Ben, he too was of the opinion that things had worked out well. Back at his base, he awaited the return of Max but it was not until shortly before daybreak that the hearse drew up outside. He and Jimmy had trussed up their captives with stout wire. Neither Rory nor Sean looked as if they had enjoyed their night out but Max had extracted the information Ben wanted from them in next to no time.

'I only had to tell that I was going to shatter their kneecaps and they became as talkative as a cage full of parrots,' he told Ben. 'Knowing that they were Irish, I reckoned that since the IRA shoot informers in their kneecaps, they would prove susceptible to that threat.

You might say that their kneecaps are their Achilles' heels,' he added brightly.

'Cut the crap! Who is paying them?'

'Seems that we are on the same side. They work for a dame called Isis who is tied up somehow with our old pal Grunwald. Do you understand the set-up, Ben?'

'I guess so.' Ben spoke drily. 'You can forget the shit about the bank owning the phallus; our employer is Isis herself. I overheard her giving orders one time to Grunwald and there is no question but that she is the boss.'

'So what was she doing with these jokers?'

'Looks as if she set them to get the girl and us to hunt the prick. I do not approve of people who play one side off against the other.'

'Why did you get into this fight, Ben?' asked Jimmy.

'I was paid to deal with Halevy. Nothing to prevent me coming to the aid of a pretty girl, was there? Oh, by the way,' chuckled Ben, 'we are now being paid by Halevy to protect his penis from Isis as well as by Isis to steal it. One or other of our clients should be satisfied eventually.'

# 9
## *Out of Africa*

When Cleo Janis was led away by Milos's guards, she was confident that the President would, on mature consideration, not carry out his threat to consign her permanently to the tender mercies of his lustiest soldiers. She was convinced that once his fury at the theft of the Golden Statue of Osiris had subsided, he would recall how sexually appetizing he had found her and that she would be restored to favour and to his bed. She was pushed into a cell and the door firmly locked. It was hot and stuffy and the only furnishing, if one could so describe it, was the bed, which was a mere stone ledge projecting from the wall, but she was alone.

The day dragged on: she was given a sordid meal and escorted to an evil-smelling lavatory by a taciturn woman guard. As the minutes and hours passed without any sign of the lecherous soldiery, her spirits mounted. Milos's outburst had been no more than a shriek of rage: powerful men were like children, subject to dreadful tantrums but which soon were forgotten. So she patiently tolerated the discomfort of her prison and somehow fought down the choking sense of claustrophobia, a condition from which she suffered agonies, by telling herself that she was on the point of being released. Consequently when the warder came to take her away, she was relieved but not surprised.

As she had anticipated, she was led back into the presence of Milos. He was sitting behind an enormous desk in his executive office. It was disappointing that the setting was so formal and Cleo was disconcerted to find that there was no chair for her so that she was obliged to stand before the desk like a recalcitrant schoolgirl before the headmaster.

Milos eyed her coldly. 'Looks like Isis has played you for a patsy,' he pronounced.

'What do you mean?'

'Get wise, shithead!' growled her erstwhile lover. 'Every scam needs a fall guy, someone to carry the can when everybody else is away and dividing up the spoils. Only this time, it is a fall girl. You, Cleo Janis, are in a tough spot. And there is nothing that bitch Isis could do to help you, even if she cared, which she doesn't.'

Cleo tossed her head back and laughed. 'What do you know about Isis? Ever since she took over from the old priestess, things have been different. There is a new vigour, a new passion, even breathing the same air as her is a thrill. Do you think that the woman who brought us to Salamba would have had the vision to carry off this raid?'

Milos looked thoughtful. Nobody had told him of the demise of the woman he thought of as Isis and her being succeeded by a new, unknown votary.

'How did the sect choose a new priestess?' he asked. 'Why couldn't it have been you? They could not have found anyone more fanatically loyal.'

'I did not have the power,' Cleo said reverently. 'I could feel that she had something supernatural, even when she was teamed up with that brute, Moriba.'

'Moriba!' gasped Milos. 'You mean to tell me that you have all fallen for that slut, Anna, the woman who was with him in Paris? Why, don't you know that she was just one of my discarded mistresses?'

'More fool you to have got rid of her. She is literally divine.' Cleo regarded the dictator with contempt and pity.

'We shall see about that,' Milos said, with a mean

smile. 'Your Anna or Isis or whatever you want to call her, she could never have planned the way that the statue was carried off, not with her bird brain! So, tell me, Cleo, who did she hire?'

'Why do you want to know?'

'Because I can use someone with his ability,' snapped Milos. 'What's his name and where can I contact him?'

'It won't do you any good,' Cleo smiled. 'You will never get back the Golden Statue, not now. We have it safe in a new shrine: it is impregnable.'

'I'm not bothered about that, you stupid cow!' Milos shouted. 'Can't you get it into your head that we are not all obsessed the way you are with some crackpot god? There is quite a different sort of job I want him to do.'

Cleo stared. Something about Milos's intensity aroused her intuition.

'You want him to get Isis,' she accused. 'That's it, isn't it?'

'What I want him to do is no concern of yours,' retorted Milos. 'Who is he, Cleo? I have to know.'

Cleo shook her head defiantly.

'Don't you understand? I am giving you a final chance to save yourself from being virtually split in half by the Presidential Guard. Once they get into you, they will kill you, and in the most barbarous manner you could imagine. Talk and you can be on the next plane out of Salamba.'

'You're bluffing,' Cleo smirked.

But she did not like the icy glare that Milos gave her as he called for the guard to remove her, and as she quit the room, for the first time, she felt qualms of misgiving. She was shoved back into the cell, and as the door clanged behind her, the smallness of the place became more oppressive than ever. It was as though the walls were closing in on her and she paced up and down to claim every inch of space. When two armed men came for her, they found her gasping for breath and soaked with sweat. Outside, the air was sweet and fresh.

'Where are you taking me?' she demanded.

The men did not answer, but led her into a single-storey structure which might have served as a stable. She was greeted by an enormous man, black as ebony, with gleaming white teeth and lips as thick as some exotic, ripe fruit. He wore the uniform of the Presidential Guard with three golden stripes on his arm.

'I am first,' he announced.

'What are you talking about and why am I here?' Cleo's voice quavered.

'You do not think that élite soldiers fuck in prison cells, do you?' The sergeant rocked with laughter. 'We have made up a roster, but we drew lots for who would go first. It was sheer chance that I won, but, of course, if I had lost we would have had another draw until the right result was obtained. It was very democratic. Now, come along.'

He dismissed the guards, and grabbing Cleo by the hand led her into an inner chamber.

She gazed at her surroundings in wide-eyed horror. At least the room was bigger than her prison cell, indeed she would have dearly loved it to have been quite a lot smaller. The walls of the long, narrow barracks were lined with a double row of two-tiered wooden bunks on which about thirty soldiers were sprawling. A few were reading books, one group of four were playing cards and the rest were looking with little evident interest at a programme on an antique black and white television set at one end of the room. The place was heavy with the fumes of cheap cigarettes which mingled with that peculiar stale, male odour which permeates all army quarters.

'OK guys, this is it. We're going to start,' exulted the sergeant.

Cleo felt every eye turned on her: the men sized her up as so much raw meat for immediate consumption. She was no prude, but she shrank away from the serried ranks of arrogant masculinity.

'Come on now, lady. This is no time to be shy,' called the sergeant encouragingly. 'Get those clothes off!'

She stood there as if paralysed, and he pulled her across to one of the bunks. Then she came to life. She crossed her hands across her breast and started to shriek. The men burst out laughing, and the sergeant began to tear off her clothes. He was much too strong for her to be able to offer any effective resistance but he controlled his violence with a display of good humour, and as she was deprived of the protection of her bra and panties, he twisted her around and displayed her nakedness for all the troop to inspect. There was prolonged applause, books were thrown aside and somebody turned off the TV. The sergeant tossed her on to the bunk and two of his comrades held her still while he removed his own pants.

'Say, ma'am, what do you think of that? Tell me now, have you ever seen a better one?'

He pointed to his rampant penis, and Cleo shuddered. It was gigantic and reminded her, in an obscene way, of an elephant's trunk.

'Stop boasting!' called another soldier. 'That thing is under-nourished. She won't even be able to feel it. Don't you fret, lady, I am Number Three and I am worth waiting for. Just bide your time.'

The sergeant had joined her on the bunk and without any preliminaries, prised her legs apart and began to thrust into her unlubricated vagina. She cried out in pain and freeing her arms from the men who had held her, she slapped him hard across the face.

'Let me go, you black beast!' she hissed.

'Racist bitch!' shouted the sergeant, and he in turn slapped her face.

'Sexist pig!' she screamed, and managed to get in one more solid blow before he pinioned her arms to her side.

All the men applauded wildly, and urged the couple on. She was dreadfully sore but she was held down by his iron muscles and was unable to stir. All the time, the man was moving over her and inside her, stifling her and crushing her, while she lay there, helpless and defeated. His hands were tight on her shoulders, bruising her skin: she tried to turn her head away but he forced his tongue into her mouth. He smelled rank and heavy, and in her ears was the rhythmic clapping of the delighted onlookers. On and on he went, and she knew that he was purposely holding himself back to prolong his pleasure in her agony. She tried to squeeze her vaginal muscles but he was so large and so strong that her efforts were futile. She prayed for it to end and quite suddenly, without any prior warning, she felt a repeated shooting sensation and he went as rigid as a corpse and then relaxed.

'Thank God,' she groaned, and she found that tears were pouring down her cheeks.

The sergeant rolled off her, picked up his trousers and hoisted them up. He smiled down at her insolently and walked away without a word. Stiffly, she climbed off the bunk, but found herself face to face with another soldier who shook his head deprecatingly and pointed back to the bed.

'No, not yet,' she pleaded.

Her protests were ignored and she found herself once more on her back, with two men holding her arms.

'Don't you worry your sweet head, lady,' her new partner said. 'I am a gentleman and have real manners, not like that rough arsehole.'

But there was nothing soothing or consoling in his

voice, only the contempt of the strong for the weak. He was perhaps a year or two older than the sergeant and smaller and stockier in build, but with an unpleasantly unkempt appearance as though his visits to the bath house were rare occurrences.

'I guess the rough way that three-stripe rascal forced himself into you must have hurt you plenty,' sympathized her new suitor. 'Now, I am altogether more refined. You suck my lollipop real good, then it will slide in nice and easy.'

As he spoke, he presented her with his fat, purple cock. Cleo found it revolting and turned her head away.

'Now, lady, don't you give yourself no high and mighty airs,' snarled the soldier, 'and if you dare to use your teeth on it,' he added as if he had read her thoughts, 'you will be torn limb from limb, but slowly and painfully. Ain't that right, boys?'

There was a murmur of assent from the rest of the troop, and Cleo resigned herself, as best she could, to the inevitable. His penis filled her mouth and pressed against the back of her throat so that she had to fight for breath and force herself not to vomit. She started to lick him rapidly in the hope of shortening her ordeal.

'Yeah, that's real nice. Keep doing that,' he directed her.

She speeded up her tongue work and the man rocked to and fro, humming to himself contentedly. She felt one of his companions jostling against them and then beginning to jerk himself off between her tits. Her mouth ached and her tongue was tired but her tactic paid off. Her Casanova was thoroughly aroused, and he withdrew from her mouth, pushed aside the man who was taking his mamillary pleasure, and plunged his saliva-soaked cock deep inside her pussy. It took only a few strokes before he uttered a hoarse shriek and emptied himself in spasm after spasm.

But Cleo had no opportunity to recover before the swaggering Number Three was on top of her. He lived up to his boast; she had never experienced anything like his massive member. She could have sworn that it was his arm, not his penis, that was violating her. Her eyes were closed and she was barely conscious as she suffered this piston, driving with unbearable force again and again, seeking her very womb. Any sexual feeling that she might have enjoyed had long been extinguished by the unrelenting abuse of her body and by the time that she had satisfied this man, she was completely emotionally numbed. She had given up all hope when unexpectedly relief came.

The men in the barracks were due to relieve other troops on guard duty, and they had to abandon their recreation in order to get themselves cleaned up before parading. Two of them took Cleo back to her prison cell, dragging her along since she was barely capable of walking.

Left alone in the dreadful dark, she lay shivering and sobbing on the bed. After only one session she was destroyed, and she knew that in the morning she would have to face the same thing all over again. And again and again. Cleo was in despair: she could not go on, but escape was impossible.

She got practically no sleep, but she was able after a while to concentrate on finding a way out of her predicament. When the guard came to give her some slops for breakfast, she asked him to take a message to President Milos. He refused. As far as he was concerned, Cleo was condemned without any possibility of reprieve, and since he was in the queue for her favours, he was not willing to do anything which might give her a chance of ending her servitude.

'You stay here,' he grinned happily. 'In half an hour, I come back to take you over to the barracks again. The boys will have finished their breakfast and should be in a good mood. The President is a busy man: he has no time for a trashy woman like you.'

Cleo had anticipated this rebuff. 'Listen,' she urged him. 'You see the skirt I am wearing?'

She pointed at the fashionably-cut tartan which she had bought in California.

'Sure,' replied the delighted guard, 'but you won't be wearing it much longer.'

'The President wants to buy one like it for his wife.'

'The President has no wife,' retorted the soldier.

'I know that,' Cleo was scornful, 'but there are certain ladies whom he calls his wife, and if you are stupid enough to offend one of them, you will be in big trouble.'

A doubt clouded the man's features. 'So what do you want?'

'Here, take this and give it to the President.' Cleo had tugged off the label from the inside of the skirt, and she handed it to the guard. 'It is the name of the boutique where he can get some like it.'

The guard examined the scrap of silky fabric carefully. It was innocent enough, concealing nothing, and he could not imagine how it could be used by Cleo to extract herself from her confinement in this one-woman brothel.

'Believe me, the President wants it.'

The soldier shrugged his shoulders nonchalantly. 'Very well. I can't see that it will do any harm, but you had better get on with your meal. You will need all your strength this morning.'

Her claustrophobia was getting worse and she was feverish. She was lying huddled and listless when the soldiers came to take her back to work. The same sergeant was waiting at the entrance to the barrack room.

'Here we are again,' he crooned. 'And I am the first.'

Cleo stared incredulously. 'But you were first yesterday.'

'That's right. We take turns, but I am always the first. I told you, we're very democratic. Now come inside.'

Perhaps Milos would be looking at the label from her skirt even now. She willed that the guard had taken it to him and that he would understand. And, in fact, the President had heard what the soldier had told him and was holding the label and examining it with a puzzled look. As Cleo had said, it bore the name of the expatriate Scottish boutique.

'Euan,' mused Milos. 'Euan, what the hell does that mean to me?'

Then he listened to the sound of his own voice, and enlightenment dawned.

'Euan, Euan. No, no, you win, you win! Clever Cleo!' He turned to a dapper major who was his aide. 'Go to the barracks of the Presidential Guard and bring the woman to me here.'

'At once, Excellency.'

The major saluted and hurried away. The guard looked on amazed until he was ordered to get out by Milos. The major arrived at the barracks at a significant psychological moment. The sergeant was in the act of enjoying the first fruits.

Cleo had hoped that she might be able to play for time, but the welcome that she was given was as peremptory as on the day before. She was not even given the opportunity to remove her own clothes before they were ripped off by eager hands.

'Don't come in while I am still dry,' she begged the

sergeant, who was stripped for action in no time. 'I am so sore.'

The man was not without finer feelings. He paused long enough to spit on his hands and to rub the saliva on to his rigid penis.

'There,' he said. 'That's better, isn't it?'

Cleo sighed, but before she could reply, she was once more tumbled on to the rough army blanket and joined by the enthusiastic sergeant. His cock seemed to have grown even larger during the night, and Cleo groaned as he forced his way into her hot, moist, but unwilling cunt. She could feel the man's mounting excitement as his speed increased. It can't be long now, she told herself gratefully, and the pain will subside. But then, oh God, there will be another and another and how many more others?

She was so intent on what was being perpetrated on her body, that she did not hear the door open as the major came into the room. The sergeant was also too occupied to notice until the officer slapped him on the shoulder.

'On your feet, soldier,' he ordered. 'The woman is to come with me immediately.'

Very few men find *coitus interruptus* an enjoyable experience and the sergeant was not one of their number. Taken completely by surprise, he leaped up and faced the intruder. But the shock proved to be the final stimulus which he required and a varitable geyser of warm sperm jetted into the major's face and gushed all over his immaculate uniform. The other soldiers in the barracks roared with laughter and shouted their approval. The well-moistened major stamped his foot in rage, put the sergeant on a charge for assaulting an officer and sentenced the entire company to extra fatigues. Then, having wrought his revenge, he escorted Cleo to the President's quarters.

Milos gave her a sour smile when they entered. 'So you've come to your senses, have you? Lucky for you that you were wearing that particular skirt, otherwise you might never have got the chance to see me. Well?'

'You will let me go if I tell you about this guy?'

'Of course. I gave you my word,' Milos exclaimed.

So Cleo told him about Ben the Bear and the ACE Office Cleaning and Decontamination Company in Zurich. When she had finished, Milos ordered the major to take her back to the villa where she had stayed.

'But you said that I could leave the country,' Cleo wailed.

'So you can when we have had a chance to check up on this Ben. And if we find that you have made up some crazy yarn just to get away, you will get worse than the Presidential Guard as bedfellows. Oh, and major,' Milos added as they prepared to leave, 'see that the lady is securely tied to the bedposts, she's into that sort of thing. Before you report back to me, please change that uniform, it is a disgrace! How dare you masturbate on duty!'

# 10
## *Honey for the Bear*

When Rory called Isis and informed her that he proposed kidnapping Sandra that night, she sent Andrew Drummond to Paris to supervise her onward transmission from the Clinique St-André. Dr Gaveau received him sullenly, but acquiesced in his waiting in the clinic for the return of the brothers and their captive. As the minutes ticked away, the Frenchman became increasingly restless, but Drummond remained unperturbed. He knew from reports from Ben that Halevy and Sandra often dined late and that Rory would not want to pounce until the streets were deserted. Nevertheless, by the time that dawn broke without any sign of the expedition returning he had become very uneasy, but there was nothing that he could do except wait.

Gaveau, being duty doctor for the night, had not gone home, but had slept in the clinic. He became aware of a hubbub outside the building and looking out, he saw that there was quite a crowd standing around a stately black hearse which had been parked clumsily in front of the clinic, completely blocking the gate. He ran out of the door, forced his way through the throng and gazed inside the hearse. Then he scurried back to Drummond's bedroom.

'You had better come and look at this,' he shouted excitedly.

When Drummond got to the vehicle, a group of male nurses were pulling the inert bodies of Sean and Rory out of the rear compartment. They were still trussed up like a couple of turkeys, ready for Christmas, and it was obvious that they both were in need of medical attention. But what attracted Drummond's notice was a note, tucked into the dashboard, addressed to Isis. He took the piece of paper before anybody else saw it, read the contents and hurried to a phone.

Isis was in her hotel suite when Drummond's call came through. She listened with annoyance to his account of the circumstances of the return of Rory and Sean and the marked deterioration in their physical condition.

'"Keep your baboons out of my way if you want results," that's what the note says and it is signed, The Bear,' Drummond told her.

'Goddamnit! Why did he have to interfere!' Isis exploded. 'His job is to get the Phallus, so why does he have to do a Sir Galahad act and rescue the damsel in distress?'

'I guess our boys were roughing up the professor, and that could have made it impossible for Ben to track down the Phallus,' Drummond suggested.

'Maybe you're right,' Isis conceded. 'You know this Ben is a pretty tough type. It was a mistake sending a couple of amateurs like Rory and Sean when we had a real professional at our disposal all the time.'

'You think you should have hired Ben to kidnap Sandra?'

'Why not? He seems to be ready to do anything as long as the pay is right. Make contact with him, Andrew, and send him to see me. I would rather handle this interview personally.'

'What do you mean, make contact?' Drummond queried. 'I've never seen the guy and have no idea where to find him.'

'Don't be such an idiot,' Isis retorted. 'It's obvious where he is some of the time, loitering about outside Halevy's apartment. And I should think that you could get a vivid description of his appearance from Sean and Rory, once they recover consciousness.'

As it happened, Drummond's task was greatly simplified when he turned up at the café opposite Halevy's apartment. As requested by Ben, the professor had arranged to withdraw the Phallus from the safe deposit in his bank, and Ben, Sandra and Halevy walked out of the front door of the block together, in full view of Andrew Drummond. There was no mistaking the identity of the alert, powerful Bear.

At the bank, the three of them were ushered into a waiting room while Halevy's authorization was verified before they were taken into a strong room and the safe deposit box produced. A bank official had one key, Halevy the other, and when both had been inserted, the box was opened and Halevy took out the Golden Phallus.

'Let me hold it,' said Ben.

He took the heavy metal rod and placed it on one palm, as if to weigh it. Then, to the surprise of the others, he produced a ruler and carefully measured the object. Taking a tiny camera from his pocket, he proceeded to photograph it from different angles.

'What's all that about?' Sandra wanted to know.

'OK, professor, put your baby back in its cradle,' smiled Ben, as he handed the Phallus back to Halevy. Then he answered Sandra: 'Suppose the worst happens and the Isis gang succeed in snatching the thing. We know that they would not melt it down for bullion, so if we have a detailed description which we could then immediately give to the police, it is possible that they would be able to recover it. It is a sort of insurance policy.'

'That makes sense,' Halevy agreed.

The Golden Phallus was consigned once more to the bank vault, and Halevy left for the university while Ben escorted Sandra home. He left her at the entrance, intending to go to the service flat which was his base.

Andrew Drummond was waiting outside the building and he called out to him. Ben regarded the stranger warily.

'It's all right,' laughed Drummond. 'I am not the Paris representative of Rentahearse, but I do have a message for you from Isis. She wants to see you at once.'

'So why didn't she come herself instead of sending that couple of knock-about comics?'

'That was regrettable,' Drummond agreed suavely. 'However, Isis will put things right. She is in Zurich. When can you get there?'

'Tell the lady that I shall meet her at the bar of the Hotel Raphael in the Avenue Kléber tomorrow at eight.'

'What, here, in Paris?' Drummond was staggered. 'You do not understand. When Isis summons, you go to her.'

'You are the one who does not understand,' replied Ben, prodding Drummond painfully in the ribs. 'I am working here, and I am not leaving Paris until I have completed the job. If she wants to see me so badly, she will be at the Raphael. See that she gets the message.'

He strode off, leaving Drummond open-mouthed, gazing after him. But when Ben reached the service flat, he found that Isis was not the only person anxious to see him.

Milos had phoned Asombolo in Monte Carlo and the Chief Minister, like the humble sergeant in the Presidential Guard, had found the call singularly inopportune.

'Let it ring, darling,' whispered Petra, and she buried her face in the shaggy hairs of his chest.

He had just that instant penetrated her and her whole body glowed at the sensation, so familiar and yet always so fresh.

'It might be important,' protested Asombolo.

'This is important,' she answered, and she emphasized

her words with that tiny twitch of her vagina which never failed to make her lover light up like a neon sign.

With a delighted gurgle, Asombolo relegated matters of state to the pending file. The phone went on ringing angrily but its sound was drowned by the music which their bodies were making. Petra was murmuring encouragement and dirty words in his ear: she had discovered that this was one of those things which turned him on. He came with one frantic drive, a moment of unimaginable, uncontrollable bliss. He held Petra firmly in his arms and covered her face with kisses.

'Jesus Christ!' he gloated. 'Honey, you sure rang the bell this time!'

On the other hand, the telephone lay still, mute and resentful. But not for long. A few minutes later it shrilled out vengefully and Asombolo picked it up.

'What the hell were you playing at?' Milos shouted. 'I don't know why you are still hanging on down there instead of getting back here to your work. So why can't you take calls?'

'Sorry, boss,' Asombolo adopted a placating tone. 'I was having a shit. And that's why I have not been able to get away from here. This European food is pure rot-gut!'

'Have you taken leave of your senses as well as of your duties?' Milos was incensed. 'Is that the way you address a head of state?'

'I beg your pardon, Your Excellency.' Asombolo had by now descended from the carefree abandon of orgasm to the reality of a servant who had been caught *in flagrante delicto* by his master. 'I should have said that I have been indisposed.'

'Well, you had better get redisposed,' Milos growled. He ordered the still-naked minister to get in touch with a concern in Zurich called the ACE Office Cleaning and

Decontamination Company and charge its head with the task of abducting Isis.

'But what is the point of that,' asked the bewildered Asombolo, 'now that you no longer have the statue in Ibari?'

'You are an idiot!' pronounced Milos. 'Don't you see that the cult will be powerless without their priestess? She is the only one who knows all that mumbo-jumbo. Grab her, and we can get the statue whenever we want it. Also, I know that woman, and I have a score to settle with her. So get this guy, Ben. He is the only man who has any idea of how to act, and pay him whatever he wants. If you don't get back to me within twenty-four hours with Ben on our books, you're fired, and you know what happens to Salamban politicians who fall into disgrace, don't you?'

The President hung up with such force that Asombolo's head was ringing.

'Come back to bed, darling,' Petra pleaded.

Asombolo stared at her hopelessly. 'Lady, I have just twenty-four hours to sign up a man I have never met or lose my head, and you talk about coming back to bed.'

'You will still have twenty-three and a half hours left,' she pointed out.

'Positive thinking!' Asombolo assented, as he got back between the sheets.

So it was that Ben found the message from his office in Zurich that the Chief Minister of Salamba was in Monte Carlo and desperately trying to contact him. He called Asombolo's hotel and was put right through: the Salamban had resolved that he would take all calls in future.

'I have this mission which I want you to undertake on behalf of our President,' he explained. 'Although he was the victim of your last exploit in our country, President Milos is not a mean-spirited man and does not bear a grudge.' Asombolo prayed devoutly that his words were true. 'When can you get here?'

'If the business is so important, you will meet me in the bar of the Hotel Laperouse in Paris tomorrow evening at seven. In case you don't know it, the hotel is just off the Avenue Kléber, directly behind the Raphael. I know you by sight: if you are not there, it means that there is no deal.'

For the second time, Asombolo had the phone banged down on him.

'Come on,' he called to Petra. 'We're checking out.'

In the service flat in Paris, Ben smiled happily at Max. 'You had better take over the watch on the prof's flat in case anyone thinks of having another try at raiding his love nest and stealing the bird. I shall have an early night: tomorrow looks like being a busy day.'

Next morning, as Halevy left for the Sorbonne, he met Ben on his way up to the apartment. He felt relieved that this sturdy, competent man would be on hand to watch over Sandra while he would be busy with his classes all day.

'Go right up,' he called to Ben. 'Sandra has just got out of bed and you should be in time for a cup of fresh coffee.'

Ben knocked at the door, and Sandra, wearing a frilly pink dressing-gown, opened the door.

He eyed her approvingly. 'Who is your dressmaker?' he enquired.

'Come on in,' she invited. 'And this is not mine, it belongs to Petra, Louis' girlfriend. She is away for a few days.'

'And you, aren't you Louis' girlfriend as well?'

'At this moment,' Sandra said purposefully, 'I am not anyone's girlfriend, and that's the way it is going to stay.'

'Do I scent singed feathers?' Ben asked with a whimsical smile.

'That's my business,' Sandra retorted. Then she threw up her hands in a gesture of hopelessness. 'Oh, hell, yes, you're right. But the guy was a prize arsehole! Come and have a cup of coffee.'

He followed her into the kitchen. He sensed an inner loneliness about her which appealed to him. On an impulse, he took her arm, swung her round to face him and kissed her on the lips. Her body went stiff, but she did not push him away. Then, as he let her go, she grabbed him and thrust her tongue deep inside his mouth. All her sexuality broke through: she thirsted for him as if he were a lush oasis in the parched desert of her life. Taking his hand, she led him into the bedroom. Maybe the oasis would prove to be a mirage, but what the hell!

He was wearing a pair of tight-fitting boxer shorts, and she tweaked them down and gazed at his vital equipment. Cupping his balls in her hand, she appraised the man.

'So, you are Ben the Bear.'

'And you are Goldilocks,' he replied, patting her soft, blonde hair.

They lay on the bed, fondling each other. She let her fingers trace the contours of his face, a strong face; reliable, trustworthy, comforting.

'First there was Daddy Professor Bear, but he was too old,' she recounted, in the voice which one would use in telling a story to a child, and she kissed Ben tenderly.

He stroked her breasts and her nipples were hard and stiff beneath his firm, sensitive hands.

'Next, there came Mummy Petra Bear, but she was too soft,' Sandra continued. She felt herself creaming, as his penis, iron hard but satin soft, moved across her flesh, and she kissed him eagerly.

'But then, she got to Baby Ben Bear, and he was just right,' she concluded, as she slipped him inside her.

And he was right. There was no trace of macho arrogance in his toughness and his love-making was breathtaking, untainted by the routine ritual which so many smug young men termed technique. He was not at all self-conscious, but fucked fluently and honestly. She was simultaneously excited and relaxed. In a word, it was simply right. The touch of his skin was good, he smelt manly and she felt as if she belonged in his arms, with him deep within her and her body responding to his. It was as though all her nerves were exposed, tingling at his every movement and she was straining for him to drain himself of every last drop of his manhood. Yet she knew he was holding himself in check, so that they could come together. She could feel that gathering storm rising from the depths of her being until the last restraints were blasted away in a wild, superb orgasm which left her shrieking, laughing and sobbing, at the very moment that she submitted to his fierce, burning virility.

She did not have to tell him how good it had been: both of them had experienced the same sensation of overwhelming joy, as though they had got to know each other in one blinding flash.

Words were superfluous, but eventually Ben did speak. 'I thought that you had promised me a cup of coffee,' he observed.

'Pig!' Sandra exclaimed with a grin. 'And I thought that you loved me for myself alone.'

When they were dressed and sitting in the lounge with their coffee, Ben regarded her thoughtfully. 'So you are a singer,' he mused. 'Do you find the work satisfying?'

'It's a living, but don't get taken in by all the ballyhoo of the pop world and the press. Most of the time, it is rushing about from one place to another, and the glamorous cabarets are hard grind.'

'I notice that you avoid giving me a straight answer as

to what you really feel about the work,' Ben commented.

'And what about you? Do you find fulfilment in being a sort of unofficial cop?' Sandra retaliated.

'I get a hell of a kick out of most of the things I do,' Ben replied. 'Of course, like the entertainment industry, the surface glitter conceals the hours of plodding labour necessary to get results.'

'So what are you, a super James Bond?' she taunted.

'You could say that.' Ben's tone was quite serious. 'And my guess is that you could make a pretty good Jane Bond, if you chose. I think you want more adventure than you get from singing sentimental ballads. What about it?'

She stared at him. 'Are you offering to take me on?'

'Why not? There's plenty of work, that I can assure you. And I am fairly good at judging people: you look like Dresden china, but you are really tough, physically and mentally, and above all you do not panic. Am I right?'

Sandra sipped her coffee and pondered this extraordinary proposition. 'No,' she said at last. 'You are right about the sort of person I am and the offer is very tempting. But as a singer, I am independent, and I want to keep my freedom.'

'Fair enough,' Ben conceded. 'But how about cooperating with me and my team on individual cases when the circumstances are suitable? You would be like an outside consultant, but I have a feeling that we would make a first class team. Don't answer now, think it over.'

Sandra nodded. 'I'd like to do that. Let's wait and see what turns up.'

The next thing that turned up for Ben was the anxious Chief Minister of Salamba at the Hotel Laperouse. Asombolo was watching the door and scrutinizing everybody who entered the lobby, calculating the probability of each of them being the mysterious Ben the Bear. He was concentrating so intently that he never spotted the man who had been in the hotel all the time, snoozing behind a copy of the *International Herald-Tribune*, in the deep leather chair opposite him.

At the stroke of seven, the stranger dropped his paper, looked hard at Asombolo and said. 'Shall we talk?'

Asombolo nearly jumped out of his skin. 'Say, man, do you always try to scare your clients to death?'

'Only when they don't pay their bills,' Ben told him. 'Now, what does the President of Salamba want?'

Asombolo made diplomatic noises, but eventually got down to proposing the abduction of Isis.

'That woman is evil,' he argued. 'We are not interested further in the statue which you took, but in restraining Isis from harming people in every country of the globe. President Milos knows her well, and believe me, he is the best man in the whole world to whom the custody of this serpent of a woman should be entrusted.'

As Milos had predicted, the suggestion that Ben should turn in his last employer was not greeted with righteous indignation. Ben's only comment was to name a price for the job which made Asombolo wince. However, he had his orders, so he weakly assented.

'But that is a great deal of money,' he pointed out ruefully.

'No priestess, no pay,' Ben riposted. 'But I insist on the money being paid into our account before we hand her over.'

'Are you inferring that the state of Salamba might not honour its obligation?' Asombolo demanded.

'Precisely. I am not a trusting type.'

'You are quite right,' the Chief Minister admitted. 'But you will have no cause for complaint this time.'

'The money should be paid to the ACE Office Cleaning and Decontamination Company,' Ben instructed him.

'That was the name which was plastered all over those vans which you sent into Salamba to steal the statue of Osiris,' gasped the astonished Asombolo.

'Sure! Have you never heard that it pays to advertise?'

So after making arrangements for future contacts, Ben sauntered out of the Hotel Laperouse to keep his appointment with Isis in the Raphael. He had no difficulty in picking her out from the mob of American tourists, Japanese businessmen and French business girls hopefully looking out for prospective clients who thronged the bar. Isis was as distinctive as a Renoir nude in a shop selling dirty postcards. Ben joined her at a small table and wasted no time in unnecessary introductions.

'I am engaged in recovering a precious object for a Swiss bank, but I presume that you have some other commission in mind?'

She regarded his mocking gaze steadily, and asked him to get her a drink. When they were seated, facing each other, she answered him.

'You know very well that I am your client already. Who other than Isis would seek the Phallus of Osiris? And, as you assumed, it was I who sent the brothers to do a little job, which they fouled up because of you.'

'Ah yes, the Undynamic Duo,' Ben said with a concerned frown. 'How are the dear boys keeping? They seemed rather out of sorts when I last saw them.'

'I don't think that they will ever be as good as new,' Isis replied curtly. 'It was a mistake using them: I want you to do what they bungled.'

'That is?'

'Bring Sandra Mitchell, alive and in fair to good condition, to an address which I shall give you.'

'The temple of Isis?' Ben asked.

'Perhaps. Or to a convenient rendezvous from where I

shall take her to somewhere suitable for what I propose to do to her. Will you do it?'

'Will you pay?' Ben demanded.

'You name your price. I have access to whatever you require. When you hand over the girl, you tell me what figure to write on the cheque.'

'It would be discourteous to refuse a lady.'

It was proving to be a bumper day for bears, Ben reflected. And it was not over yet, he told himself, judging by the way Isis was looking at him.

'I have checked in here,' Isis said. 'Why don't you come up to my suite where we can have dinner together and get to know each other better?'

'It would discourteous to refuse a lady,' Ben repeated.

They ordered a meal and told each other a series of fictions about their past lives, but everything about this man confirmed her initial impression.

'So let's cut out the shit that Grunwald was feeding me.' Ben was suddenly serious. 'Why is this Golden Phallus of such earth-shattering importance?'

Isis decided to come clean with him, at least up to a point.

'It has erotic, some would say, magical properties. Attached to the statue which you so dashingly pirated out of Salamba, it would be the centre of quite marvellous rituals over which I would officiate.'

'I can imagine,' Ben murmured. 'But how did you get the job?'

Isis stared at him unhappily. 'Tell me, do you think I am pretty?'

'No,' he answered without hesitation. 'You are beautiful.'

'Exactly. I am beautiful, so I was selected. The men and women who worship me are my slaves, but I myself am no longer free. I have become their slave. Being a goddess is a lonely profession. Do you know what I want now more than anything else in the world?'

Ben shook his head. 'Tell me.'

'To be loved as myself, a woman, not some mythical creature.' She got to her feet and brought over the cedar casket. 'With the aid of this little box of tricks, I could play such games with you that you would be reduced to a mere sexual robot, believe me. But there is not one man in whose arms I can lie, and with whom I can make love simply as myself.'

'What about the dignified British gentleman who approached me?'

'Andrew Drummond!' she laughed bitterly. 'I could never trust him. He is the most vicious creature I have ever met. He killed my predecessor, although I pleaded for her life, and I was forced to watch him exult in her death throes. Have you any idea of how sadistic a doctor with a blood lust can be? No, I need a man on whom I can rely, someone strong, masterful yet considerate, and above all, someone who has not been contaminated by the loathsome lust which this damnable cult of Isis propagates like a plague.'

Ben was amazed by the violence of her outburst: he saw the tears spring to her eyes.

'And you, my fine bear, could you bring yourself to make love to me?' Isis asked in a voice which was torn by emotion. 'Are you the man for whom I have been looking, or are you just like all the others; false, cruel, weak and treacherous?'

It was one of those questions which cannot be answered by words. Ben took her in his arms and held her close as if to reassure her that they were still ordinary human beings. She kissed him passionately.

'Come,' she whispered, 'show me what it means for a real, living woman to be loved by a real, living man.'

She was as beautiful as a dream with her clear blue eyes yet delicate dusky skin, a woman in whom were combined the classic loveliness of Europe with the torrid sultriness of Africa. And making love to her was an immersion in an icy fire. The cedar casket lay disregarded in the salon while the two of them explored the wonders of their bodies in the adjoining room.

Ben laid her on the bed and kissed her smooth, enticing flesh from her raven black hair to her perfectly formed toes. There was not one flaw in the whole of her radiant body, and he embraced it with the gentle strength of a man who was not afraid to give himself in the supreme act of love. And she was a woman of flesh and blood herself, not some echo of a creature long dead. Her voice in his ear was as soft as the murmur of a distant sea, but it raised him to a fever pitch of desire.

'That is so good,' she spoke huskily, 'to be with you, to be able to let myself go and know that at last I have found a man I can trust. Not to have to keep up my guard, even when I fuck. This is paradise!'

Ben said nothing but closed her mouth with a kiss which left her moaning and gasping. Their bodies were joined as if there were no force on earth which would be strong enough to tear them apart ever again, and in their orgasm there was the fury of wild beasts and the gentleness of angels.

Yet, unbelievably, it had to end, and Ben prepared to leave. She did not want him to go, but with an ironic smile, he reminded her that he had work to do for her, for which she was paying him. He kissed her goodbye, a lover's kiss.

'Come back soon, my lovely, big, grizzly,' she called, as he left the room, but when he was out of earshot, she added contentedly, 'there's plenty more honey waiting for you in my bear trap.'

# Part III
# Climax!

# 11

## *Wet Dream or Nightmare?*

'You are a shit, kidding me that Milos was coming to Europe,' Petra shouted down the phone.

'If you were so disappointed, why have you not come back?' Halevy replied angrily. 'After your last performance here, I would have thought that you would be keen on seeing Sandra again, even though you are so annoyed with me.'

'I have stayed on in Monte Carlo because something has turned up which should be very much to your advantage, although I do not know why I bother with such an ungrateful bastard.'

'Is that so?' The disbelief in Halevy's voice was perhaps justified, since Petra was calling him from a hotel in Paris Asombolo had checked into as soon as he had concluded his meeting with Ben. 'And have you managed to secure the golden statue from Milos's representative?'

'Yes, there are no problems about that, but I will tell you the details later, when I see you.' Petra glossed over the fate of the statue, and she did not tell Halevy that it was no longer in the possession of Milos for the simple reason that Asombolo, fearing that such a revelation might cut short their acquaintance, had not told her about the raid on Ibari.

'I need to know now because Professor Khalid is coming to Paris. You remember that he is the curator of the National Museum of Egypt, and I am going to meet him in a couple of days' time.'

'Listen, Louis,' she interrupted hastily, 'you have always said that as long as that Isis woman is roaming about, neither we nor the Statue of Osiris, and above all the Golden Phallus, will be safe.'

'So?'

'Well, this nice Mr Asombolo is arranging to get rid of her, for once and all.'

'Seems an unlikely assignment for the Chief Minister of a country,' commented Halevy. 'And he needs your presence in this enterprise?'

'Don't sneer, Louis. Of course he won't carry out the snatch himself, but he has brought in a spectacular hit man. And as for me, I shall be the bait to lure Isis out into the open. Asombolo has done his homework on the lady, and he has found that she is a voracious lesbian. So get your Khalid to sit tight and wait.'

'It seems that I don't have any choice,' Halevy grumbled, and the conversation ended without the usual exchange of endearments.

If Halevy had known that Asombolo's agent was none other than his own trusted Ben the Bear, he might have begun to have some doubts and these would have been greatly increased if he had then discovered that it was the same Ben who had carried off the statue from Ibari.

Halevy repeated to Sandra and Ben what Petra had said and suggested that, as she gave no clue as to when she would be returning to Paris, perhaps Sandra should return to Britain, but Ben vetoed the idea.

'If and when Isis is finally out of the way, or when the Phallus is safely in the custody of some museum, you can come and go as you please. But until then, if you are to remain under my protection, I want you to stay together here in Paris. Do you mind too much?' he asked Sandra.

'Not at all. I don't have any engagements fixed for a while, and I am quite enjoying my unplanned holiday,' she answered.

She could have been more precise and said that it was those morning sessions with Ben after Louis had gone off to the university which gave her such unalloyed pleasure, but she considered that to say so might hurt Halevy's feelings.

'Why don't you show Professor Khalid the Golden Phallus while he is in Paris?' Ben suggested.

'I have already thought of doing that, provided you can give me one or two of your men for protection.'

'Do you know where he will be staying?'

'Egypt is a poor country, so Professor Khalid will be spending a few days at the Plaza Athenée.'

'That figures,' Ben agreed. 'It is still one of the most expensive spots in the city. You go ahead and take the Phallus for him to see: I personally will ride shotgun for you.'

While preparations were being made in Paris for the Golden Phallus to have its outing, Isis had returned to Zurich where she was discussing another phallus with Grunwald.

'I thought that you said that Ben the Bear was with the Mossad,' she accused. 'He isn't even circumcised!'

The banker considered the evidence. 'It's probably some sort of disguise,' he ventured.

She decided to ignore this inanity. There was so much to be done in the light of Ben's latest report, and Grunwald was sent away with his head buzzing from the welter of orders he had been given.

Now that she was sleeping regularly with Ben, Sandra found less zest in her nights with Louis Halevy, but he appeared to be content with their rather more placid relationship. However, the night before he was due to extract the Golden Phallus, he was unusually restive and ill at ease. Sandra wondered whether it was her fault, perhaps he sensed that she was preoccupied with another man, and she felt guilty. Hell, she told herself, I have no reason to reproach myself: I don't belong to the man, and we can still be good friends. But though she tried to persuade herself that it was irrational, the feeling that she was betraying him persisted.

So when he held her in his arms, she was more responsive than ever. They kissed as though they already knew that this would be their last night together, and Louis took her with the breathless wonder of a young virgin boy suddenly finding himself in bed with the woman of his impossible dreams. He had never been so gentle, nor she so loving. Their sex was an enchantment, awe-inspiring and mellow; the sweetness of spring and the ripeness of autumn brought together in one final embrace. Even orgasm came as a quiet fulfilment, an almost sad conclusion, like a hushed twilight at the end of day. His fingers stroked and fondled not only her breasts and her buttocks, but also the delicate curve of her neck, the subtle swell of her belly and the fragrant golden filigree of her pubic hair. His hands bade her farewell as did his tongue when he took his last sip of nectar from her mouth and from her vagina. They made love in silence; Sandra's cheeks were wet with tears when they moved apart and Louis was racked by that prescient grief and sense of loss. She had a sensitivity which he had never found in Petra, even when they were most in harmony. Theirs was a melancholy joy.

The next morning, Ben came by to go with Halevy to collect the Golden Phallus. The professor was surprised that they went by taxi, but Ben explained that he had arranged for a car to be waiting for them when they came out of the bank with their precious consignment.

'Goodbye, sweetheart,' Halevy called to Sandra as they left. 'I might be a bit late back; I have a lot of things to talk about with Khalid.'

'I won't worry, since you are in such good hands,' she replied, with a knowing smile to Ben.

Before going into the bank, Ben looked around. Parked

outside the bank was a black limousine with a man sitting in the driving seat.

'What's that parcel?' Halevy asked, pointing to a cardboard carton which Ben was carrying.

'It is some jewellery which I have just collected for a client, but I won't be able to deliver it for a few days. As a matter of fact, it is rather valuable: do you mind if I leave it in your safe deposit box here?'

'No problem,' Halevy answered. 'Just let me know when you want to pick it up.'

The safe deposit box was handed over, and Halevy took out the Golden Phallus. He went to the counter to sign a form of withdrawal, leaving Ben to put his own parcel into the safe deposit box and hand it back to the bank official.

'I unpacked my stuff so that we could use the carton for the Phallus,' Ben told Halevy as they left the bank. 'The jewels will be perfectly safe inside the safe deposit box, and we could not have you parading around the streets of Paris with an exposed golden prick, could we?'

They walked across to the car. The man had moved into the back seat, and Ben took his place behind the wheel. Halevy went to sit beside Ben, but he motioned him to join the stranger, who smiled genially at him. The car moved off.

'So let's see this fabulous object,' demanded the stranger.

Halevy frowned, but Ben, who had carried the parcel out of the bank, tossed it to him. He opened the box and gazed at the chunky rod of gold. Halevy glanced out of the window.

'Which way are you going?' he asked Ben. 'You should have taken the Avenue Montaigne. Don't you know where the hotel is?'

But Ben ignored him, and the car swung on to the Boulevard Périphérique and joined the traffic heading out of the city to the north. By now Halevy was thoroughly alarmed.

'What's going on? Where are you taking me?' he shouted.

'Please, do relax, professor,' urged Andrew Drummond. 'When Isis arranged for the delivery of the Golden Phallus, she particularly asked that you should accompany the package.'

'You treacherous bastard, Ben!' Halevy hissed. 'And you are stupid, too. Hasn't it occurred to you that when I don't turn up at the Plaza Athenée, Khalid will call the apartment to find out what has happened to me and that will alert Sandra? The cops will be out after you before you can get clear of the city.'

'I don't think so,' said Ben. 'Khalid got your message that you were hoping in a few days to get hold of the entire statue of Osiris and that he should wait for you to contact him. I don't think that he will be either alarmed or displeased at the opportunity for a few more days in Paris – and a few more nights!'

'What message? I never sent any message.'

'No, it slipped your mind, so I sent one in your name,' Ben informed him.

Halevy relapsed into baffled silence. The car picked up speed once they joined the autoroute and headed towards Lille. Before midday, they were approaching the Belgian frontier. Drummond had removed a hypodermic needle from a case, and he held it close to Halevy's wrist.

'I don't expect there to be any trouble in crossing this frontier,' he said pleasantly, 'but in case you were considering trying to attract the attention of the police, I would strongly advise you against it. You see, the needle has been tipped in curare. It is a poison which acts almost instantaneously, and it is very painful.'

'Louis, the guy is a killer,' Ben warned him.

However, nobody on the frontier wanted to see their

documents and they were waved across without stopping.

'You know Belgian cooking is excellent,' Ben remarked. 'It is a pity that we have too tight a schedule to be able to stop and sample some. Maybe next time, Louis.'

'Have a ham sandwich,' Drummond invited. 'I brought a few along for the trip, a sort of picnic lunch. I assure you that they are absolutely wholesome. I am going to have one, and you can choose whichever one you like.'

He offered a packet to Halevy, who ignored him.

'Please yourself,' sighed Drummond, 'but do let me know if you change your mind. Otherwise you will get awfully hungry.'

He helped himself to one, and passed another to Ben. The two men munched contentedly while the car sped northwards. At Breda, they crossed into Holland and Halevy tensed himself while the Dutch frontier police examined their passports. He saw with dismay that Ben had handed them three, one of which must have been a specially prepared forgery for him. Nobody could accuse Ben the Bear of lack of careful preparation.

It was dusk when they drove into the outskirts of Rotterdam. For a while they followed the signs for the huge Europort, but then branched off until they came to one of the smaller canals which linked up with the complicated network of waterways at the mouth of the Rhine. It was a bleak scene; the last rays of the watery winter sun on the oily grey water of the canal. There was a rotting wooden jetty, flanked by drab functional warehouses, and tied up beside the jetty was one of those long narrow barges which stream up and down the Rhine, carrying every sort of cargo known to mankind. The car stopped and Drummond pushed Halevy out. He and Ben escorted him up the gangplank and into the barge. A woman, muffled in a fur coat against the chill, regarded him with an amused smile.

'Welcome on board the *Firebird*, Professor Halevy,' said Isis.

Halevy blinked. He could not believe his eyes; this had to be a bad dream. But what made him doubt the testimony of his senses was not the sight of the woman whom he recognized as having been the companion of Moriba when they burst into his apartment, disturbing as that was, but the twin apparitions beside her. The first was a tall gangling man who might have been almost any age. He boasted the most imposing bald head that Halevy had ever seen, a sort of miniature of the dome of St Peter's, but ringed around with tufts of bright red hair. His equally flamboyant beard was trimmed to a point in the approved imperial style and the singularity of his appearance was further enhanced by the fact that one of his eyes was greyish-blue while the other was brown. The effect was completed by the man's dress, a long, dark blue frock coat with gold shoulder epaulettes and brass buttons, worn over baggy Cossack trousers and calf-length boots. He glared at Halevy as though he were a particularly unwelcome cheese mite.

'I am the master of the *Firebird*, the Grand Duke Alexei Fyodorovich, but you may address me simply as sir,' he announced. The solemnity of this statement was diminished by the fact that his voice was a quavering treble and his accent heavy and guttural.

The man who was standing beside this august personage snorted derisively. 'The stupid old sod is crazy as a coot,' he informed Halevy. 'I am the mate, my name is Frank, and if you misbehave, I am the guy you will have to reckon with.'

In striking contrast to the Grand Duke, Frank was built like a house, all brawn and muscles. He was about thirty and his face was one immense scowl. By way of uniform, he wore a greasy, rough seaman's jersey and heavily-stained blue jeans. Grime appeared to have been etched into his face and hands and sprayed on to his clothes.

The *Firebird*'s skipper's face was contorted with fury, but the dispute between him and his insubordinate mate was cut short by Ben addressing Isis.

'The fee payable to the ACE Office Cleaning and Decontamination Company covered the delivery of the Golden Phallus. The subsequent amendment of the contract to include the person of Professor Louis Halevy naturally will entail a supplementary payment.'

'I thought he came as a bonus,' protested Isis.

'I shall stay on board until the additional money is in our bank account.'

'I rather hoped that you would,' said Isis. 'There is quite a pleasant double cabin. Alex, stow the professor away in some secure corner of this tub.'

Halevy was hustled into a tiny cabin which might have passed as a padded cell, but for the fact that there was a window of thick glass which looked out on to the narrow deck of the barge.

'And what is a grand duke doing on a canal boat?' enquired Halevy, as the captain led him to his prison.

'My father was the Grand Duke Fyodor Oblomov. Our estates around Kiev ran to thousands of square kilometres and at one time we had more serfs than anybody other than the Tsar. So when he died, I succeeded to the title.'

'Don't you believe him,' called the mate. 'His old man drove a taxi in Paris.'

'Of course he did,' the captain flared up. 'That proves my story is true: all the taxi drivers in Paris were Russian archdukes, or at least dukes.'

Halevy considered that explained the way so many Paris taxi drivers handled their vehicles. But once inside his cell, he turned his very considerable intellect to assessing his own situation and his prospects. He was certain that if he fell into the hands of Isis, he would either be killed or reduced by means of her unique combination of black magic, hypnosis and drugs to a state of utter mindlessness. He was pretty sure that the man who had sat beside him in the car was a doctor of some kind or other from the professional equipment in the case from which he had produced the hypodermic, and his obvious familiarity with the objects. Yet he was not completely without hope. He had heard Ben say that he was remaining on board, and he remembered his promise to ride shotgun for him when they were about to leave the flat. He had hired Ben on a hunch, and men always hope that their hunches will work out. Maybe, despite appearances, Ben was keeping a watchful eye on him after all. And surely, if he were a captive for any length of time on the *Firebird*, all sorts of people would become alarmed and start a search for him. There would be Sandra and Petra, as well as Khalid and his own colleagues at the university. No, provided the bizarre crew of the barge did not dispose of him into the muddy water, there was still hope of rescue.

But Petra was a doubtful ally, he decided. She was clearly as keen as mustard to hop into Milos's bed and Halevy still believed that the statue of Osiris was in Ibari, and that the President and Isis were working together. So the destination of the Golden Phallus must be Salamba, and presumably that was where they intended to dump him, if he survived the journey. He guessed that the barge would drop him and the Phallus close to some deserted spot where a plane could land to sneak them out of Europe.

He would have been much less sanguine if he had been able to listen to a conversation which Ben had with Sandra. The boat chugged its way up the canal, but it had stopped again at a small town where Ben was able to use a phone.

'Where the hell have you got to?' Sandra demanded. 'I

was hoping that the three of us would go out this evening, perhaps with this Khalid character.'

'Don't worry,' Ben reassured her. 'There's not just Khalid but a whole gaggle of archaeologists here, and we are meeting up with the guy who has promised Petra the entire statue of Osiris. This is likely to take some days, but I shall keep my eye on Uncle.'

'But I'm lonely,' Sandra pouted. 'I want you now; why can't you be here?'

'I miss you too,' Ben told her, 'but if you ever want to be a good Jane Bond, you must learn to do as you are told. Why don't you go to a movie or read a good book? Improve your mind, your body is perfect. Now, in the morning, look outside at the terrace of the Café l'Univers. You will see a nice young man in a brown raincoat, reading *Le Figaro*. His name is Max, and he is one of my men who are making sure that you don't get into any trouble. If you want company, go to the café and take a drink. Carry that book which I left in the apartment, *Sexual Deviations in Micronesia*, and make sure that Max sees it. He will come upstairs ten minutes after you leave the café. Treat him gently, he is a pure, unsullied soul and should not be corrupted.'

'So when are you going to pick up that slut?' asked Isis, who had listened in to the call.

'After we have got rid of this cargo,' Ben replied. 'We do things in my time. Now, there are a few more people I must talk to.'

The following day, a notice was posted in the Sorbonne informing students that Professor Halevy was indisposed and would be absent for several days, while Khalid learned that his old friend was now quite hopeful of his being able to obtain the entire statue of Osiris, and Halevy entreated him to wait patiently for developments, according to the message which was left at the desk of the Plaza Athenée.

That night, Ben slept with Isis, the Grand Duke Alexei slept with Frank, but Halevy was accompanied only by his doubts and misgivings. Andrew Drummond also spent the night on board the *Firebird*. Alone with Isis, to whom he had handed over the Golden Phallus, he chuckled drily on learning of the sleeping arrangements. 'So you are going to weave one of your spells around the big strong bear, are you?'

'Not at all,' Isis rebuked him. 'He is man enough to be able to satisfy a woman without the need of any artificial stimulus. And don't you understand that I need one man who can make love to me as an equal, not as a slave whom I have reduced to a slobbering idiot? But the guy has to be something special, which you, my devoted Andrew, are not.'

Drummond was furious, but he did not have the courage to contradict her, so he stormed out and went to his cabin which was next to Halevy's padded cell. Both men were soon to be regaled with a grotesque spectacle.

Alexei and Frank required a lot of space for their sex games, in fact the entire run of the deck. What brought both Drummond and Halevy to their windows were the hoarse screams of the noble Russian. The captive had suspected that the gallant mariners were gay when he first set eyes on them, and this impression was confirmed by the exploratory grope of his arse by the master of the vessel when he was being escorted to his cabin. Later, he was brought some rolls and cheese and a mug of black steaming tea by Frank, so obviously the butch partner, who stopped to pass a few observations.

'That bloody old fairy is cracked about ballet. That's why he called the boat *Firebird*. Have you ever heard anything so ridiculous? I wanted to name it *Gay Crusader*, but he said that there was nothing left to crusade about, and we had to celebrate the genius of Diaghilev. Even the bloody cat is called Petrouchka. He'll have you in a tutu before the end of the voyage, probably tripping the Dance of the Sugar Plum Fairy.'

'Where is the end of the voyage?' Halevy wanted to know.

'I don't know where your voyage will end, and I would not tell you if I did.' Frank leered unpleasantly and stomped out of the cabin, locking the door behind him.

But when the fun and games started, Halevy and Drummond witnessed an amazing reversal of roles. The grand duke, still wearing his uniform of a high functionary in the Tsar's service, was going for a ride in his droshky. He was seated in a heavy wooden sled, brandishing a wicked-looking whip and urging on his steed. Frank, naked and crouching on all fours between the traces of the sled, galloped along the deck, making gruff, barking noises. Halevy guessed that Alexei was insulting his human quadruped, and spurring him on to greater efforts, but since he was shrieking in fluent Russian, he had to judge by the frenetic tone of his treble voice. The weird pair rushed past his window and their mingled screams and barks could be heard all over the vessel. By the time they had completed their third circuit, the scene had undergone a transformation. By tugging relentlessly on the reins, the rider had pulled the sled so close to the sweating, howling mate that their bodies were in contact. With an unearthly shout, Alexei, who had dropped his Cossack pants, leaped on to his man-dog's exposed arse and virtually speared him with his erect penis. The ride was over and on the open deck, the captain set about fucking Frank with bestial fury.

'Bravo!' shouted Andrew Drummond from the next cabin. 'What is this, the Carnival of the Animals?'

Alexei was too intent on driving his cock hard into Frank to answer such facetious questions, but when he had squeezed the last drop of his semen into his partner, who rolled over on the deck as if he had been pole-axed, the captain turned to face the cabin windows.

'That was an additional *pas de deux* which I devised for *The Rite of Spring*,' he announced proudly. 'But Stravinsky objected. That one, he had no vision, he did not know genius when it was before his short-sighted eyes. My great uncle, Vladimir, he was the first man to make love to Nijinsky on the stage. It was a beautiful, experimental ballet, but he was too far ahead of his age. Rasputin threw a pumpkin at his head. That one, he had no soul!'

The captain emphasized his point by spitting demonstratively: the mate crawled away, and quiet returned to the good ship *Firebird*.

In the comfortable double cabin, a more conventional act of love was being celebrated.

'Now don't you dare to complain that you are too tired,' Isis warned Ben, as she unbuttoned his shirt.

'As long as you don't try and pull the fragile female with a headache routine,' he countered.

However, by the time she had got down to unzipping his trousers, it was obvious that no excuses would be necessary. Her eyes flashed a challenge that whatever his sexual achievements, she would match them.

'Come to the grand duke's imperial-sized bed,' Isis invited. 'His excellency has graciously yielded it to us for the night. He will be slumming in the mate's bunk.'

'Is there anything in this aristocratic crap?' Ben asked, as he followed her to the captain's unchaste couch.

'Who cares if it gives the old crackpot a kick? But he surely knows how to live the part. Look at that bed!'

Any less self-assured lovers than Ben and Isis would have been utterly overawed by the bed. It was nearly as wide as the boat itself and it stood on elegantly-wrought legs, decorated with gilded angels. Above the ornate headboard stood a carving of a crowned eagle.

Ben had removed all his clothes and Isis looked at his tanned muscular torso with relish. She sank to her knees and took him in her mouth. He tasted as good as he looked, and she found that the more she feasted, the greater was her appetite. She got to her feet and took him by the hand.

'Come to bed,' she proposed, and she led the way on to the vast structure.

'Take off that thing,' Ben ordered.

Isis was crouching before him, naked apart from the tiny ribbon of her bra. She shook her head. 'I always wear something when I make love.'

'Not with me,' Ben insisted. 'That is for your slaves: you turn them all into fetishists. Remember the way it was in Paris and show me that you know how to give love as a real woman.'

He pulled off the offending slip of nylon. Isis sighed, and submitted. Ben stroked her thighs and then let his fingers roam over all the enchantments of her body. He played with her toes, massaged her calves, kneaded her arms and fondled her firm, full breasts. She knew him with every inch of her body even before he very gently pushed her on to her back, eased open her legs and sank his head in between them.

His lips and his tongue were an ecstatic torment, delighting and provoking her. It was as though she had within her womb a raging furnace and every movement of her lover fanned the flames of her lust until she was being consumed by a white hot passion which she could no longer restrain.

'Fuck me now, now!' she implored.

He moved over her body deliberately so that she felt the rough stubble of his chin against the tender flesh of her belly and her firm breasts with their erect nipples. His lips locked on to hers and their tongues met in a honeyed embrace. She felt herself gushing uncontrollably over his rigid penis which penetrated and possessed her. It was all so right. She lost all sense of time and space: nothing existed outside their two bodies, so closely intertwined that they moved, breathed and lived as one. She squeezed her muscles around his unyielding cock, which thrust remorselessly within her, and the pressure on her red, ripe clitoris was driving her out of her mind. She could not stop, but she willed him not to come until she was ready for him, and somehow he held back. It was as though the fire inside her was spreading, swelling, taking over every fibre of her being, until it burst in one wild moment of culmination which brought him also to the explosion of his climax. They lay, panting like savage beasts, but motionless in the after-death of orgasm.

But he was indefatigable and she was insatiable. Hardly had they spent themselves, before they were once more fused together. Isis was not simply a woman any more, but the female half of this wonderful new creature into which they had been transformed by their union. The sun was beginning to tinge the dark waters before, finally conquered by sheer exhaustion, they relapsed into slumber.

Halevy also had slept little, but his night had been passed far less agreeably. When it was light, he looked through the window and was able to see that the *Firebird* was no longer in the confined waters of the canal. A procession of ships steamed past them, and on the banks, lines of cars and trucks made their way along highways. Houses and factories were clustered all around the waterway: Halevy realized that they were sailing up the Rhine.

Frank brought him a frugal breakfast and in sullen silence refused to answer his questions. Still, he thought, it is morning and I am alive. If they had wanted to throw me overboard, surely they would have done it during the night in some deserted spot. And somewhere on this accursed boat, there was Ben: was he possibly riding shotgun?

In the archducal cabin, Ben sipped his coffee and gazed thoughtfully at Isis.

'So what are you going to do with the professor?' he asked.

'Oh, he will have the time of his life,' she smirked. 'He will be the star performer in a ceremony in the new temple of Isis, together with that little bitch of a Scottish singer, when you bring her to me. They are lovers, aren't they?'

'I guess so, why?'

'Well, they will make love just one more time, at the feet of the statue of Osiris, and at the conclusion of their ritual, my faithful worshippers will sacrifice them. They cannot be left alive, you understand; they know too much and they could recognize too many faces.'

Ben nodded. 'And where is this great new temple where you are putting on the show?'

Isis smiled. 'That remains my secret, my darling bear. I trust you absolutely when you are in my bed, but outside I believe in caution. We shall agree a spot where you will turn this Sandra over to me. I shall pay you, and there your involvement with the business will end. OK?'

He shrugged his shoulders. 'Suit yourself. Who am I to object as long as you pay up as promised?'

Later that morning, Halevy saw the twin spires of Cologne cathedral as they glided past. They look like a couple of Golden Phalluses, he told himself with a bitter smile. Then, in the suburbs of the city, the *Firebird* made for the shore and he watched as the boat tied up beside a small jetty. He waited, but nobody came for him. There was a clatter of a gangplank, and he saw Ben stride off the boat. A man came to meet him and handed him a piece of paper. Although Halevy was unaware of it, Grunwald was handing over the agreed payment for delivery of his body. Ben pocketed the cheque and turned to walk towards the city. He waved his hand cheerfully, but was he saying farewell to the prisoner or to her captor? Either way, as the *Firebird* headed once more down river, Halevy knew that now nobody was riding shotgun.

# 12
## *Lechery–Treachery*

The President of Salamba was in a foul temper. It was time that his Chief Minister was back in his office, dealing with all the affairs of state which were either being left in abeyance, mishandled by incompetent junior ministers or, worst of all, dumped on the President's desk. The last message from Asombolo had confirmed that he had made contact with the formidable Ben the Bear and that he had accepted the commission to deliver Isis to Milos. Impatiently, the omnipotent dictator tried for the umpteenth time to place a call to the hotel in Paris, and found himself talking with a dentist in Milan. He would have to get the national telephone company to replace its outworn equipment, he told himself, and he grimly resigned himself to waiting for Asombolo to get round to calling him.

In fact, Asombolo was being kept busy. Petra, he had discovered, was a most demanding mistress, and he was suffering from lack of sleep. Also, he was aware that he could not hang on indefinitely in Paris and he was not looking forward to his reception by Milos when he ultimately limped back home. He had just been on the point of pouring himself his breakfast whisky and Petra was calling to him to come back to bed, more a command than a request, he noted ruefully, when the phone rang. Saved by the bell, he congratulated himself, as he picked it up. Even a call from the wrathful Milos would provide a short respite, but the voice was not that of his master.

'If you are serious about taking a certain Egyptian deity back to Africa, you had better arrange to have a private plane standing by,' Ben told him.

'When can you deliver?'

'Who knows?' Ben answered cheerfully. 'But be a good boy scout and be prepared. I know that you must find the weather in France ghastly after all that marvellous sunshine back home, so we shall try to make your stay as brief as possible.'

'Don't let that worry you,' Asombolo replied. 'My personal comfort is less important than your getting results.'

'I wonder how you manage to pass the time?' The concern in Ben's voice did not sound the least sincere. 'And, one last thing,' he added. 'You had better get your arse out of Paris: I suggest that we make the pick-up point for your fancy goods Geneva. I can let you have the name of a pilot with his own plane who is the soul of discretion and is prepared to fly out any sort of cargo to anywhere in the world.'

'What's keeping you?' Petra called from the bedroom. 'I need my man!'

'Get packed,' replied the reluctant stud. 'We're leaving.'

So while Asombolo looked forward eagerly to Isis being handed over to him, Isis herself, with the same keen sense of anticipation, awaited the delivery of Sandra. Halevy, on the other hand, viewed the future with understandable foreboding. Ben had vanished, and with him his last forlorn hope of rescue. Isis had also gone ashore to supervise the preparations in the temple for the reception of the sacrificial victims as well as the Golden Phallus, which she left on the *Firebird* rather than run the risk of smuggling so suspicious an object herself into Zurich. The complement of the boat was now entirely male although not entirely masculine.

During the afternoon, he received a visit from Andrew Drummond who solicitously checked his temperature, blood pressure and general health.

'We must have you in top class condition for your gala

appearance, mustn't we, old chap,' he confided. 'Everybody would be dreadfully disappointed if you put up a lack-lustre performance.'

'What precisely do you and the rest of your gang of crazy criminals intend to do to me?' Halevy demanded.

'Don't take it like that,' Drummond expostulated. 'After all, there are lots of people who pay good money for a cruise down the Rhine. And where else would you find a skipper like our Alyosha? I am sorry that I cannot enlighten you on the nature of the ceremony which Isis is planning, except to say that both you and your girlfriend will play leading roles.'

'Girlfriend?' Halevy echoed fearfully.

'Yes, indeed,' Drummond beamed jovially. 'The tartan lassie who sings and whom you left in your flat. She is being picked up at this very minute. So you need not fret: you are going to have congenial company. See how kind and considerate Isis is!'

Halevy was silent. He realized that any appeal to Drummond would be pointless and only add to his tormentor's sadistic pleasure at the helplessness of his captive.

'But talking about putting on unusual shows, I am sure that you must have been amused by the gallivanting of the grand duke last night. He had a word with me just now, and he is rather hoping for your cooperation in this evening's session. You see, he has for a long time had an ambition to drive a troika around the *Firebird*. His droshky act is only a one-horse sleigh, but the prospect of having three racing steeds under his lash has him drooling with sexual excitement. Frank would of course be lead beast in view of his seniority and his being familiar with the routine. He invited me to be second string, as it were, but I was obliged to refuse: I don't think that the council of the British Medical Association would approve. However, he has pressed into service a horny young seaman who will do most things for money, and that leaves just one more horse to be broken in. So I have volunteered your services, rather than let the poor old freak die of a broken heart.'

'I'll do no such thing,' Halevy flared up.

'Steady on,' Drummond rebuked him. 'I thought that you would be pleased to get out of this stuffy cabin for a bit, and the exercise will do you good. Speaking as unofficial ship's doctor, I must insist that you join in the fun and festivities. Can't have you going broody.'

'That lunatic is a friend of yours?' Halevy was intrigued by the connection between the suave London doctor and the demented White Russian barge-master.

'Let's say an acquaintance. I operated on him when I was working for a spell in Paris. He had been to the Opéra to see *Swan Lake*, a lovely but difficult ballet, don't you agree? Back home, he tried to run through some of the dance steps himself but when he attempted a particularly complicated *entrechat*, he tore some tendons and made quite a mess of his leg. Afterwards, when he found that I am something of a balletomane myself, he was so pleased that he kept in touch with me after I went back to London. He was always suggesting that we should get together and form a new company to put on the revolutionary ballets of his great uncle, Vladimir, the one who was given the raspberry, or rather the pumpkin, by Rasputin, you remember.'

'I see,' Halevy commented unsmilingly. 'And I presume that your venture was so great a success that he bought this boat with the profits.'

'Glad to see that you have kept your sense of humour,' Drummond replied. 'Of course I did not finance the stupid old fart. His driving was so erratic that he was obliged to sell his Paris taxi, the insignia of the Russian nobility. Luckily for him, his father had got a lot of the family jewels out of Russia after the Revolution, so he had the cash to put down as a deposit on the *Firebird*. He had started this affair with Frank, and that is how he was persuaded to take to the water. But his heart remains in the ballet, so you won't let him down tonight, will you? I gather that the backing music will be by Prokofiev, the Sleigh Ride from *Lieutenant Kizhe*. I am looking forward to a sparkling display, a choreographic triumph.'

Drummond went out, leaving Halevy wondering how he could avoid the musical ride, harnessed beside two malodorous seamen for the delectation of the Grand Duke Alexei, or Alyosha to his intimate friends. But a more serious worry soon overrode this all too personal consideration. Was Drummond's statement that Sandra was being gathered into Isis's net true, or was it just a bluff which he had dreamed up in order to add to Halevy's mortification?

In fact, once he was satisfied that he had jolted Asombolo into motion, and that Petra was still with him, Ben had turned his attention to Sandra. She had found no difficulty in picking Max out from the other men who haunted the Café l'Univers, although she had not felt so much at a loss as to invite him up to the apartment. Consequently, she was surprised when he presented himself at the front door.

'Ben sent me,' said Max, by way of introduction.

'Where is he? Is he all right: I mean, nothing has happened to him, has it?'

'No need for alarm,' Max hastened to calm her doubts. 'Can I come in?'

'Yes, of course,' Sandra answered apologetically, and led the way inside. 'Can I get you something, a drink or a coffee?'

'I'd sell my grandmother for a cup of tea,' Max confessed. 'I've been stuck in that infernal shanty across the road for what seems like a lifetime, condemned to drink their coffee. I think that they must brew the stuff from pulverized prickly pears and strain it through a sweaty sock.'

'It does have a distinctive flavour,' Sandra assented. 'So, tell me what your lord and master has to say to me while I make you a cup of the elixir of life.'

'Your dear old Uncle has gone off on the spree with a whole band of bone gatherers, mummy collectors and such-like pursuers of the past, dragging poor Ben along with him. It appears that they're going to be closeted in serious conference for some days, probably discussing what toothpaste Cleopatra used or whether the pyramids are really Martian space ships. Ben knew that you would be pining for him, so he sent me to collect you to come and join him and save him from dying from boredom. You can spare a couple of days, can't you?'

'I'm not doing anything particular here, waiting for Louis to get back,' Sandra replied. 'How is Professor Halevy?' she enquired: Max surely deserved a mild snub.

'He is his usual sprightly self,' Max said blithely. 'Now, why don't you go and pack a case, while I imbibe the cup that cheers.'

'Where are we going?' she called from the bedroom.

'Germany. Koblenz, to be precise. Ben is waiting for you there. And before you ask me why this egg-headed conclave has congregated in such a pestilential hell-hole, let me tell you that they have got themselves a romantic castle on the Rhine somewhere outside. At Koblenz, I hand you over to Ben: he always reserves the nice, juicy jobs for himself. I am a mere hewer of wood and a drawer of water, as the good book says.'

'Did you go on talking like that in the Café l'Univers? If so, I am not surprised that they gave you the dregs from the coffee pot.'

Max shook his head sadly. 'You are like all the others, blind to my sterling virtues. I shall wilt away in some desert, unappreciated to the last. Aren't you ready yet? I was hoping that we could get to the airport before the worst of the traffic. You don't have to take a whole trousseau, you know.'

'Coming.' She staggered back into the room, lugging a suitcase.

Max groaned. 'I only brought a sports car, not a bloody pantechnicon. Here, let me take it.'

Outside, a trim white Mercedes was waiting. Max wrestled her case inside, complaining all the while of his multiple hernia, then wound a silk scarf round his neck, pulled on a checked cap and donned a pair of stylish leather gauntlets.

'This was the uniform which my father wore,' he explained. 'He was a great fighter ace in the Second World War.'

'Which side was he on?' asked Sandra.

'That depended on who he was talking to, and what he was trying to sell.'

Max was a good driver, despite all his easy banter, and Sandra was perfectly relaxed as they weaved through the trucks and taxis, heading for Charles de Gaulle. But Max left the highway shortly before the turn-off to the main airport.

'Ben has a light plane standing by at Le Bourget,' he explained.

Sandra would not have described the twin jet Mystère as a light plane and it annihilated the distance to Cologne, where another fast car was waiting to whisk them to their rendezvous. Max chattered away, but when she tried to obtain some hard information from him, he proved to be evasive.

'Tell me about Ben and your set-up. Where does he come from?' she asked.

'Let's not talk shop: it's so boring,' Max moaned.

Throughout the journey, he managed to steer the conversation away from any discussion of him or Ben but he listened attentively to what Sandra told him about her own life and career. By the time that they drew into the courtyard of the Hotel Lorelei, a few kilometres beyond Koblenz, and she had joined Ben in the bar, her knowledge of the history of the two men was as fragmentary as when she had set out.

'Glad you could make it,' Ben said, and he kissed her chastely on the cheek. 'I hope you like the hovel.'

As hovels go, the Lorelei was quite exceptional. Part of the building dated back to the fifteenth century when it had been constructed by a Graf von Pegnitz, a Franconian nobleman who was locally more powerful than the Emperor. It was a great, gloomy fortress, dominating a stretch of the Rhine above its junction with the Moselle. Later, when its function as a castle had ended, a more hedonistic von Pegnitz had drastically modified the place, turning it into a dignified country house, virtually a miniature palace. Now it was a luxury hotel, its rooms giving on to a spectacular vista of the river.

'Where is Louis?' Sandra asked Ben, as the three of them took a snack at the bar.

'He's gone for a trip on the river with some of his chums,' Ben replied. 'You can join him shortly, but I thought that we might have a little time to ourselves first.' He turned to Max. 'You have a long drive ahead of you, so you had better get going.'

Max looked even more morose than usual, put on his fighter pilot outfit and got to his feet.

'Good day, Miss Mitchell,' he said to Sandra, with all the dignity of a retiring ambassador. 'It has been a pleasure: I trust that we shall meet again soon and have the opportunity to further our acquaintance.'

'Piss off, Max!' Ben cut short his farewells, and Max stalked out.

'Time for lunch?' Ben proposed.

'Time for bed,' Sandra amended.

However, to her surprise, Ben insisted that they ate first. 'I am just as keen as you are,' he stated, 'but we have to be realistic. You have not had a meal since Paris, and it may be a lot longer than you think before you have the chance to eat again.'

So they went into the dining room and in spite of Sandra protesting that she was not hungry, at least not for food, Ben ordered a substantial lunch for them both. Such was his charm and consideration that Sandra rapidly recovered from her immediate disappointment over his order of priorities. Only after they had taken their brandies and coffee, did he consent to lead her upstairs.

The room which Ben had taken was spacious and airy with a balcony poised above the river bank, and sunlight streamed on to the cream-coloured coverlet of the double bed.

'It's been such a long time,' sighed Sandra, as Ben took her in his arms.

'Nearly two days.' he smiled.

'That's what I said, a hell of a long time.'

He took off her clothes as if she were the most precious and the most fragile object in the world. The marvellous thing about Ben, she reflected, was the way that he always made her feel how much he wanted her and somehow he seemed instinctively to know not only what to do to her, but the precise moment to do it. With Donald, she had invariably been the one who took the initiative; it was good to be able to let herself be led by a lover, at once strong and sensitive. His hands were just right, and her skin glowed beneath his touch, while his mouth was sensuality itself.

'Be nice and gentle with me today,' she urged.

'Any way you want it,' he murmured, and kissed her long and lovingly.

He took the wine of her lips and nibbled and licked her tender, lustrous flesh and she accepted the tribute of his body. When he went down on her, she knew what heaven would feel like.

'I bet James Bond couldn't do it so beautifully,' she chuckled.

'That's because he did not have such a sexy Jane Bond,' Ben assured her.

'Don't speak. My mother told me that every time you talk you lose a mouthful,' Sandra upbraided him.

The sucking, slurpy sounds from between her legs bore witness to Ben's approval of her mother's worldly wisdom. He was doing fantastic things to her clitoris and that familiar, wonderful sensation was spreading through her entire being. She knew that she would soon come, and she wanted him deep inside her. Her hands stroked his ears and his cheeks, coaxing him to raise himself and take her. His penis was magnificent, so hard, so exquisitely shaped, so utterly desirable, and it was hers. She pressed him into the very depths of her, while he folded her in his arms. He was moving faster and faster, both of them were gasping for breath, and then they came together like a sunburst. She could feel him pouring out his seed, the very essence of the man, and it was as though the wild quaking of her vagina was drinking in every last drop of his semen. If only time would stand still, and they could remain for ever, each a part of the other!

But they did at last move apart. Sandra went into the bathroom to clean up: as she returned, she looked out of the window at the majestic river and the throng of shipping moving past in both directions.

'Isn't it strange that so many of these boats fly flags which are so much alike,' she said to Ben, who was stirring himself from the bed.

'What do you mean?'

'Well, look. They are all three stripes of one sort or another. The German stripes are horizontal, and over there are a couple of Dutch and French barges with their vertical stripes.'

'Tricolours,' Ben corrected. 'There are a few other designs, like the white cross of Switzerland, but yes, you are right, most of the shipping on the Rhine fly flags of similar design with three colours. What on earth set you thinking about flags, a couple of minutes after we have made love?'

'It was that strange flag on a boat which has tied up outside the hotel. Come and look: I've never seen anything like it before.'

Ben walked over to the window and burst out laughing. The craft which had caught Sandra's attention was, very correctly, displaying at her stern the red, white and blue tricolour of the Netherlands. But from her mast, there fluttered a broad, square flag, depicting the imperial black eagle of Tsarist Russia. The *Firebird* was hardly inconspicuous.

'This is a funny place for a barge to put in, isn't it?' Sandra queried.

Before Ben could reply, the phone rang.

'I'm back,' came Max's voice, 'and the gang's all here.'

'We'll be right down. I'll meet you on the river bank.' Ben replaced the receiver and turned to Sandra. 'Let's go and inspect your mysterious barge. I gather that it is the boat on which Uncle Louis and his playmates have had their mini-cruise.'

They dressed and went downstairs, and as they walked out of the hotel, Ben took Sandra by the hand and spoke in a low, earnest voice. 'Strange things are always happening to Jane Bonds, you know, so you should never let the unexpected faze you. Can you keep your head?'

She was puzzled, but she answered, 'I guess so. Why?'

Ben led her up the gangplank of the *Firebird*. The Grand Duke Alexei popped up from behind the bridge, and she gasped in amazement. She was so intent on the bizarre appearance of the captain of the *Firebird*, that she did not notice the small party who had approached the gangplank from the river bank and were now coming on board.

'Where is Louis?' she demanded.

'The good professor is in his cabin. I shall lead you to him shortly.' It was Alexei who answered, accompanying his words with a graceful bow which would have been a credit to Nureyev.

'Nice work, my noble bear,' exulted Isis, as she and Grunwald stepped on to the deck of the barge. Sandra made a dash for the gangplank, but was held back by Max, who brought up the rear of the group. She stared in alarm at Ben, but he was concentrating on Isis.

'Our transaction is not yet completed,' he observed.

Isis snapped her fingers, and Grunwald advanced and handed Ben a cheque.

'That seems to be satisfactory,' said Ben. 'I understand that the lady is going to be well treated on the voyage?'

'That is not your business,' Isis laughed. 'But, of course, we shall cherish her until she can be offered up to Isis and Osiris at the due time and in the proper place. Now, bear, back to your den!'

'Is it true, do they have Louis here as well?' Sandra cried out to Ben.

'Isn't that touching! Such selfless devotion!' commented Andrew Drummond, who had come on to the deck from his cabin. 'Yes, your dear friend is nice and snug, although I must admit he does not seem to be enjoying the trip as much as I would have hoped.'

'Let her see the old arsehole,' Isis jeered. 'But keep them in separate cabins and don't let them talk to each other.'

'You double-dealing shit!' Sandra called to Ben as she

was pushed down the companion-way. The last thing she heard was Isis suggesting to Ben that they meet again soon on a more intimate occasion and his enthusiastic assent.

# 13
## *Lust's Labours Lost*

A cabin had been prepared for Sandra on the other side of the *Firebird* from that occupied by Halevy, but Drummond made sure that she was taken past his cell. Since the inboard cabins had quite wide windows instead of portholes, she was clearly visible to him and she was able to make out his melancholy features before being half-led, half-dragged away by Frank, under the scornful gaze of Drummond.

Isis and Grunwald, having witnessed the successful conclusion of Ben's double abduction, left the boat and made their way back to Zurich where they both had a great deal to do, Isis in the preparation of the temple and Grunwald in finding ways of concealing the substantial payments which the bank had made on behalf of Isis from the scrutiny of accountants and auditors. Max and Ben had already driven off in the opposite direction: the Grand Duke Alexei ordered Frank to cast off, and the *Firebird* resumed her progress down the river towards Switzerland.

Heavy storm clouds were gathering, and to the fury of the captain, as the darkness descended, so did the rain. However, it could be said that the downpour provided the only ray of sunshine for Halevy. Frank, swathed in oilskins, brought him a mug of greasy tea.

'There'll be no Ride of the Valkyries for Alyosha tonight,' he announced. 'This storm has set in: he'd need a stable of seahorses for his moonlight caper.'

At least Sandra would be spared the spectacle of him careering naked round the deck, dragging the terpsichorean tar, and that gave him a crumb of comfort. The disconsolate grand duke stamped into Sandra's cell and his odd-coloured eyes gleamed malevolently, as if it were her fault that the heavens had opened and deprived him of his troika ride. Maybe there was fresh talent here, awaiting discovery.

'*Sur les pointes!*' he commanded.

Sandra stared at him uncomprehendingly.

'He wants you to stand on tiptoe,' explained Frank, who had followed the captain into the cabin.

Before she could comply, Alexei strode over to her and pinched the calves of her legs, with the air of a butcher assessing the quality of a side of beef. With a sigh, he turned away. 'Do not bother,' he called in a mournful, broken treble. 'You do not have what Pepita called the musculature. It would take years of training at the barre to toughen the sinews. You are too flabby even for a back-row little swan in the *Lac des Cygnes*.'

'You will be heartbroken to hear that you have failed to qualify as a fledgling ballerina,' Frank sneered. 'If you can't dance, you will be expected to fuck!'

The two men left the room and locked the door behind them. Sandra began to have doubts about her own sanity. But despite the mate's threat, she was left unmolested.

The *Firebird* pushed its way steadily up river and so it was that shortly after Asombolo and Petra had entered Switzerland from the west at Geneva, Halevy and Sandra entered from the north at Basle. Halevy recognized the city on the great bend of the river and a flash of lightning lit up the mediaeval cathedral with its multicoloured tiled roof. He knew that the river ceased to be navigable for vessels as large as the *Firebird* about here and he wondered what diabolical scheme Isis or Drummond had thought up to get their two captives through the Swiss customs post.

The pulse of the engine slackened as the barge proceeded at half-speed and then dead slow. Through the murk, wharves and warehouses could just be made out, and the *Firebird* tentatively nosed her way alongside a quay. There was the slightest shock and the noise of the ropes being fastened to the shore bollards, then silence. Nobody attempted to land from the vessel, and no one on land had any inclination to get drenched boarding her. Whatever the nature of the barge's freight, it would wait until the morning.

However, no sooner had Halevy resigned himself to spending another night on board, than a new distraction occurred. An armour-plated bullion van with a motorbike escort of half-a-dozen men in police uniforms drove on to the quay. Four burly security guards from Grunwald's bank dismounted from the van, strode up the gangplank and clattered on board. There was the sound of voices, the guards in Swiss German, Frank in Dutch and Alexei in a shrill hotch-potch of English, French and Russian. The door to his cell was thrown open, and Halevy found himself being hustled in the middle of a group of men off the boat. He had no chance to make a break for it, and there was nobody nearby to whom he could call for help. The authority of the bank was such that the customs and immigration officials were prepared to let the guards get on with the job of unloading the cargo, whether it be precious metal or human bodies, and the master of the *Firebird* could sign the necessary forms in the morning. The unfortunate Egyptologist was pushed unceremoniously into the back of the van, and a couple of guards climbed in behind him. A minute later, the door was opened and Sandra stumbled inside. He noticed that one of the guards was carrying the box into which Ben had stuffed the Golden Phallus: he presumed that it would be declared to the customs as bullion which was being consigned to the bank. What could be more natural? He looked hopelessly at Sandra as they heard the key turn in the lock, and the van moved off. All that their arrival in

Switzerland had achieved for them was to exchange a prison on the water for one on dry land.

'Louis, are you all right?' Sandra asked anxiously.

'Yes. So far, nobody has physically assaulted me, but I guess that our luck has run out, thanks to that treacherous bastard, Ben.'

'I would never have believed that he would turn out to be one of the Isis gang,' said Sandra. 'Where do you think they are taking us?'

Since the bullion van had no windows, Halevy had no notion of what route they were following. He shrugged his shoulders. 'I suppose there is some deserted airfield or landing strip where they will bundle us into a plane and take us to Salamba.'

Sandra shuddered. She had experienced Salamban hospitality during the events which led to her smuggling the Golden Phallus out of that country and she did not look forward to a return trip.

'It stands to reason,' Halevy continued. 'Isis is in Ibari: she must have done a deal with Milos, and the statue of Osiris is there. Now they have got the Golden Phallus, the last fragment of their idol, God knows what sort of witches' sabbath they plan to stage.'

'And what happens to us?'

'At the period of the original statue of Osiris, the Egyptians had abandoned the practice of human sacrifice,' Halevy propounded. 'I am very much afraid that these infernal devil worshippers will not take the trouble to make their ceremony historically authentic.'

'What you mean is that they will kill us?'

'That is one way of putting it,' he admitted.

Sandra laughed sardonically. 'Cut out the academic gobbledygook! What other way is there of putting it?'

The van had stopped several times, and Halevy deduced that they were in a town where the procession was halted by traffic lights. He was not prepared, therefore, when the rear door of the vehicle was flung open and he and Sandra were hustled out into the road.

They were in a narrow side turning, just round the corner from a broad, busy street. Although it was now late at night and the heavy rain was still falling, there were cars, people and trams, one of which was passing, its bell clanging and blue and white pennants fluttering from the top of the cab. They had literally no more than a second to register this scene. The van was standing outside a tobacconist's shop, its door wide open, and they were bundled across the narrow strip of pavement and inside by their guards. They were pushed past the counter and through a door at the back of the shop.

As they were escorted down the long corridor, Halevy was able to whisper to Sandra, 'We are in Zurich. Did you see that street car? They all fly the flags of the canton, blue and white.'

'Great! What good is that nugget of information going to do us?'

Halevy looked forlorn, but he was also puzzled. What the hell were they doing in a subterranean passage in Zurich? He was still wondering when they were once more separated and confined in cells which were little more than cupboards. They were only a few metres away from the theatrical setting of the temple of Isis.

As for Sandra, the blackness of her mood was as much due to the shock of her betrayal by Ben as to her predicament. She had trusted him absolutely and when they had lain together in bed, she would have considered it inconceivable that he would do anything to harm her. And yet, all the time he must have been calculating the precise manner in which he could most effectively get her, Louis and that damnable Phallus into the hands of Isis. And she had fallen for all that nonsense about James and Jane Bond! What a laugh he must be having at her expense. Well, she reflected, after this, she would never be so gullible as to put her faith in any man again, no matter how smooth his line of patter. That is, of course, if there was going to be anything after this. With an effort, she turned her mind away from pointless recrimination of the bear who had turned into a serpent. Louis had been quick enough to see that they were in Zurich, and that provided her with the tiniest glimmer of hope. If, by some miracle, during whatever ritual Isis had in store for them, she were to get the chance to make a break for it, at least she would be in a civilized city, surrounded by normal men and women among whom she would be able to seek refuge. And that was a damned sight better than finding herself in Ibari or the Salamban jungle where the population would be hostile, or at best indifferent.

Cleo Janis would certainly have shared Sandra's opinion of Salamba. Milos had been as good as his word and had allowed her to fly out of Ibari, from where she had hurried to Zurich to find Isis and to let her know that she had been obliged to divulge the identity of Ben the Bear to Milos, and her suspicion that his purpose was to hire Ben to hunt down Isis herself. However, Isis had been out of town and it was only in the early afternoon following the day of Halevy's and Sandra's capture that she was able to catch up with her in her hotel.

'Christ! You look a mess.' Such was Isis's greeting to her handmaiden.

'So would you if you had been through what I have,' Cleo complained, and she proceeded to give a blow by blow account of her ordeal.

'I expect that you had the time of your life,' Isis replied, with more humour than sympathy. 'Now, get yourself cleaned up. We have a big day ahead of us.'

'I went to a lot of trouble to come to warn you of the danger that you are in,' said Cleo resentfully.

But her alarm over Ben the Bear being hired by Milos was dismissed by Isis with derision.

'You don't know what has happened while you were busy enjoying yourself, entertaining the studs of the Salamban army,' she said with a smile. 'Ben is my man. Yesterday, he delivered the professor, the singer – and the Golden Phallus. I have them all. Get it into your head, the game is over. We have won, and whatever Milos might have had at the back of his mind, he is too late to touch me. Ben has been paid off by Josef Grunwald; he was expensive, but he certainly got results. I expect that he is relaxing after a strenuous few days, sitting in an easy chair watching an old-time western movie on television, or taking things easy in some country cottage with a girlfriend.'

Cleo looked dubious, but Isis tossed her head impatiently. 'Get moving, Cleo. The ceremony in the temple is due to start in an hour, and I have to get ready. Make sure that you are not late.'

She was not the only person to receive a brusque invitation. Grunwald had called an immediate board meeting and he informed his colleagues that they were to attend the ritual in the bank vault. One or two of them bleated protests that they had important engagements, but they were silenced by Grunwald.

'It is the direct command of Isis,' he rapped out. 'I am sure that you do not want to risk her displeasure. Remember your last experience in the temple.'

The directors were cowed. They recalled with shame, and in some cases pain, the weird events of that evening. A number of these respectable pillars of the banking community were still too sore to be able to sit down on a hard chair.

During the afternoon, men and women presented themselves at the tobacconist's shop round the corner from the bank where they showed their medallions before being admitted into the corridor behind the counter. In their cells, Halevy and Sandra heard the constant procession of footsteps and they realized that their nightmare was approaching its climax.

In the temple, the assembled ranks of the followers of Isis and Osiris waited for the arrival of their priestess, the incarnation of the goddess. From hidden loudspeakers solemn music blared out and the battery of lasers played over the glittering torso of Osiris, and on the newly-mounted head of the statue. Even the most sceptical onlooker would have found the scene impressive. For the faithful, it was overwhelming. The board of directors huddled together in one corner, as much in thrall to the strange power which seemed to emanate from that immobile object from the past as the most impressionable youngster.

When Isis herself entered, there was a reverent hush. She was dressed in her splendid robes, on her head was the double crown of Upper and Lower Egypt, and on either side of her, attendants carried symbols of her authority; a crook and a whip. In her hands was an incongruous brown cardboard box. All eyes were on her, as she set the box down on an altar-like table, and triumphantly drew out of it a great rod of gold which she displayed to the multitude. There was a roar of delight.

'The Golden Phallus of Osiris!'

Halevy heard the tumult, and shivered: Sandra, in her own cell, steeled herself for what was to come. And, unknown to them, a whole fleet of cleaning vans began to move across Zurich.

Isis raised her arms, and the crowd in the temple fell silent. 'Our quest is accomplished,' she declaimed. 'As from today, all the mighty powers of the ancient gods have returned to the world. The time has come to spread our message to every nation. When the devotees of Isis and Osiris are numbered in their millions, they will not be able to congregate in this one temple, the heart of our cult. So today, our celebration of the restoration of the great statue will be recorded: I have ordered the installation of video recorders and each of you will receive copies of the tapes which are going to be made. Then, I order you to go back to your respective countries and to start the work of establishing chapels for local worship. You will succeed, because backing you up will be the irresistible force which will radiate from this temple. We have the wealth to reach out into every home, and you have the power – the power of lust!'

The shouts of approval echoed through the vast cellar and cameras zoomed in on the figure of the priestess and the wonderful wand of gold in her hands. A group of young men and women, selected for the outstanding beauty of their bodies, took up their places in front of the statue of Osiris. The music changed to the savagely sensual 'Dance of the Seven Veils' from Strauss's opera *Salome*. The youths commenced a fantastic dance, a memorial in movement to sexuality. As the music grew louder, the rhythm more insistent, their miming became more abandoned, and they discarded the richly-coloured silk clothes which had emphasized the contours of their bodies, but had become mere restraints. The enthusiasm of the performers was infectious: one after another the spectators stripped and gloried in the nakedness of their bodies. Isis had meanwhile laid the Golden Phallus on the altar, and had taken the familiar papyrus from her cedar casket. As she uttered her invocation, her voice was amplified so that it blended with and eventually dominated the lush strains of the orchestra.

Halevy heard the music and found little comfort in recollecting that the central theme of *Salome* was how carnal lust culminated in human sacrifice. His morbid consideration was disturbed by the arrival of two big muscular men who grabbed him by the arms and lugged him out of his cell and into the maelstrom of bodies in the temple. Turning his head, he saw that Sandra, struggling furiously, was being manhandled behind him: both of them were thrown to the ground before the statue of Osiris, and at the feet of the proud priestess.

The scene was astounding. Never in her life had Sandra seen so many virile men and voluptuous women, all in fast and furious action at the same time. The music was deafening, and the unearthly chanting of Isis was having its customary effect, breaking down all inhibitions and driving the celebrants to unimaginable excesses. She saw frenzied women seizing men and gobbling at their genitals; homosexuals and heterosexuals mingled without any distinction. It was a case of anything goes – and everything went!

Halevy's head was spinning from the din and the stifling heat which had built up in the confined space. Out of the confusion emerged a figure which he recognized. Andrew Drummond had shed his formal suit as inappropriate garb for such junketing, and he had somehow laid his hands on a leopard skin with which his serious-looking spectacles with their tortoiseshell frames made an odd effect, like a caveman from Fifth Avenue. With him was Cleo Janis, resplendent in a costume which appeared to consist entirely of spangles. Drummond held Sandra, while several of the male dancers tore at her clothes until she was nude. Halevy had no opportunity to interfere, or even to protest, since he was undergoing the same treatment at the hands of a group of wild young women, under the direction of Cleo Janis. She pushed him in the direction of Sandra.

'Go on, man,' she urged him. 'Fuck her good and hard because this is positively your last appearance in public, or in private.'

'Are you out of your senses?' screamed the outraged academic. 'Don't you know that there is no evidence of human sacrifice in Egypt during the dynasty whose conditions you are so inaccurately attempting to recreate?'

However, to his chagrin, the participants in the orgy had no interest in historical authenticity, and his objection was greeted with coarse laughter.

'You puny creature!' Isis shouted. 'Can't you get it into your thick head that we are not evoking the past, but making the future? This is the dawn of a new age of Isis and it will be consecrated by your copulation – and your death.'

'What she really means,' Drummond whispered confidentially in his ear, 'is that you both know too much. Now be a good fellow and do get on with it; have a good time.'

Halevy wanted to stand firm and refuse to cooperate but he saw to his horror that he was sprouting a healthy erection and that nothing he could do would cause his mutinous member to shrink. Could it be that Thanatos, the dark god of death, was so close a neighbour to Eros, or was it the insinuating music, the resumed chanting of Isis and the defiant display of irrepressible animal lust by all around him that was destroying his self-control, and his ability to survive?

Sandra fought to contain her mounting panic which threatened to reduce her to sobbing hysteria, but she too was unable to withstand the onslaught of rampant sexuality all around her. Drummond smiled at her encouragingly.

'Be a good girl, if you will excuse the misuse of the term, and do fuck the gentleman. Otherwise, we shall merely cut your throat in front of him, and I am sure that he would find that even more distressing than the quite sensational conclusion of your intercourse which we have planned. Believe me, in deciding the circumstances of your farewell orgasm, due weight has been given to a consideration of your feelings, as well as the desirability of adding zest to the innocent pleasure of these good folk.'

They were pushed together and they held each other

tight to find strength and comfort in each other's arms rather than to satisfy the blood lust of those around them. But the appeal of the flesh could not be denied and, against his conscious will, Louis Halevy felt his wild penis, as though it had a mind of its own, pushing between Sandra's soft, wet thighs.

The last van of the ACE Office Cleaning and Decontamination Company drew up outside the tobacconist's shop.

'It has to be here,' said Ben the Bear. 'OK, boys, let's go!'

Officers in a cruising police car noticed that a no entry sign had been placed at the entrance to the street, and were mildly puzzled. They had no information on any road works which were about to be started, and it seemed odd that a street in the very centre of the city, although very small, should be closed to traffic in the busiest hours of the afternoon. There were no signs of any disturbance, but there was an unusual profusion of vans from a local company, drawn up outside a shop. If this had happened round the corner in the Paradeplatz, in front of one of the great banks, there would have been cause for alarm, but here it merely evoked curiosity. So the two policemen did not stop and investigate, but they were sufficiently aroused to report the closure of the street by their radio to police headquarters.

'We're closed,' growled the man behind the counter in the tobacconist's shop.

'Pity,' commented Max. 'That's bad for trade.'

The grouchy shopkeeper did not reply, since by now he was lying unconscious on the floor. A whole posse of cleaners and decontaminators swarmed into the shop and forced their way into the corridor. However, part of the force were busy pulling equipment from the vans, the most conspicuous items being a series of heavy wicker hampers, like those used for transporting theatrical costumes. At the end of the underground passage, they came to a sturdy door which should have been manned by another sentinel. But, since he could rely on being alerted by the man in the shop in the event of an emergency, he had left his post in order to watch the fantastic ritual which was being enacted inside.

At police headquarters, the report from the patrol car was acknowledged, and passed to the duty officer. He was at that moment tied up with a bomb scare at the Central Station, so the matter had to wait for a few minutes before he could turn his attention to it.

Those inside the temple were oblivious to all that was happening outside. Everybody was intent on the spectacle of the tender yet passionate coupling of Sandra and Louis, as they signed their death warrants with the sinuous sensual movements of their limbs. They were so perfectly attuned to each other that their bodies responded, one to the other, without any conscious effort or thought. So complete was their harmony that if the Grand Duke Alexei Fyodorovich had been present, he would have enrolled them unhesitatingly to play the leading parts in the avant-garde masterpiece of his great uncle, Vladimir. Both of them wanted to hold back, but the very peril of their situation was a goad, driving them inexorably towards their fatal climax. Halevy told himself that what was happening was impossible, yet there he was, with the fragrant body of Sandra in his arms, fucking as if his life depended on it, rather than the exact reverse.

He was becoming delirious. The faces around him were no more than an undifferentiated blur, the music a meaningless jangle of sound. The only reality was the woman who was clinging to him. Even the air seemed to be charged with a swirling white mist, and bustling among the followers of Isis were strange figures with faces like frogs. That was when he lost consciousness.

'You had better send a patrol car to see what is going

on in that street,' the duty officer told the radio operator in headquarters. He had successfully dealt with the bomb scare which turned out to have been a false alarm. By the time that the signal was received, the original car was a couple of kilometres away from the Paradeplatz and the side street. They drove around a block and headed back in the direction from which they had come. Since headquarters had delayed so long before responding, they assumed that there was no urgency and consequently they did not disrupt the traffic and upset the good citizens by racing back with siren howling, but proceeded calmly and sedately.

There was nothing calm and sedate about the actions of the operatives of the ACE Office Cleaning and Decontamination Company. Those of them who had donned gas masks and released the gas which had previously proved so effective in Salamba were rushing in and out of the temple, bringing out inert bodies which their colleagues dumped into the hampers which were then loaded into the waiting vans. It took a matter of minutes to clear the vault of every living creature.

The police car had been held up at a couple of traffic lights, and when it reached the side street, the road sign had disappeared, and so had the fleet of vans. It all looked quiet, but the conscientious upholders of the law sauntered into the shop to make quite sure. Minutes later, they were relaying the incredible news of a tunnel leading into the vaults of one of the leading banks. There was pandemonium, but strangely enough, not one director of the bank could be located. However, a senior manager checked, and confirmed that nothing was missing. The evening newspapers reported complacently how the vigilance of the police had frustrated an attempted sensational bank raid.

# 14
## *A Phallus-y*

Following the instructions which they had received from Ben, Petra and Asombolo had checked into the Intercontinental at Geneva. Petra would have preferred one of the older hotels down by the lake, but Asombolo insisted that they should be as near as possible to the airport where he had to meet the pilot who was prepared, so he had been assured, to spirit him plus an unidentified woman passenger out of Switzerland to Salamba. The meeting took place, a bargain was struck and the Chief Minister returned to the hotel to await developments.

He found Petra in a tetchy, irritable mood. He offered to take her down town to do some shopping, but she refused. She was equally uninterested in a trip on the lake. Since the storm which had so disrupted Alexei's projected nautical sleigh ride in Basle had now reached Geneva, Asombolo had to admit that the prospect of heaving about in a steamer on the choppy, wind-tossed water, peering at the grey, mist-shrouded shore through the sheets of lashing rain, was somewhat lacking in charm.

'Have a drink,' he suggested hopelessly.

'I don't want a bloody drink,' Petra retorted. 'You think that alcohol is the answer to everything.'

Scenting that a row was fast brewing, Asombolo poured himself a stiff whisky. 'Is something bothering you?' he asked timidly.

'You could say that,' Petra replied. Her tone was cold, but there was venom lurking beneath the surface. 'Let me ask you two questions. First of all, why is it that whenever I want to go to bed, you think that it is time to go shopping, have a meal, watch a movie, drink yourself paralytic, in fact do anything, except make love? And secondly, instead of haring off to Geneva on some wild-goose, or wild-witch chase, why are you not arranging with Louis for the delivery of the statue of Osiris from Salamba? You must see that you are putting me on the spot. I have to explain to him what I have been doing for Christ knows how long, when I was supposed to be negotiating with you for the damned thing.'

Asombolo swallowed hard: the moment of truth had arrived. 'I have a confession to make. We don't have the statue.'

Petra stared at him.

'It's true. God knows where it is now, but it was stolen by Ben the Bear for Isis. I did not want to tell you sooner: I thought that if you knew and told Halevy, that would bring this relationship of ours to an end.'

'You mean that all this time, you have been playing me along?' Petra stormed. 'Why, you two-faced, double-dealing arsehole!'

Asombolo pondered how an arsehole could be two-faced, but decided that it would not be politic to pose this semantic conundrum to Petra at this juncture. Instead, he attempted to divert the tempest which was raging around his head more furiously than if he had been outside at the mercy of the wind and rain.

'Come to bed,' he invited.

'I wouldn't go to bed with you if you were the last man on earth.'

'But a minute ago, you were complaining because – '

'I've changed my mind,' Petra interrupted.

'But I love you,' wailed the disconsolate minister. 'Please, Petra, baby, don't be unkind. Think of the good times we have had in the past few days. And the only reason I didn't tell you was so that we could be together for a little longer. Don't spoil our last few hours.'

His appeal was so piteous that Petra's anger was

dissipated. After all, she reflected, there was something in what he said, and he did have a stupendous cock.

'Oh, hell,' she relented. 'Come on, then, but you are still an A1 shit.'

So on this occasion, it was Asombolo who led her into the bedroom.

'And I expect the full treatment.' Petra knew when to press home her advantage. 'Show me just how much you do love me, all of me. I'm not going to settle for just a couple of rubs of my tits as though they were Aladdin's magic lamp, a cat's lick at my clit, and one quick poke to finish, all in five minutes flat. Understood?'

Asombolo silently prayed for the stamina to complete the gruelling course along which he had originally cantered with such delight. But by the time that the two of them were lying in the bed, his old enthusiasm began to return. What better way was there, when all was said and done, of passing a wet afternoon in Geneva? Or anywhere else.

The last of his lady's petulance was massaged away, as his hands worked assiduously over her shoulders and ran lasciviously down her back. Halevy, Ben the Bear, Isis, all of them could wait until her senses had been sated by her man's hands and mouth – and that great, tasty, black cock!

Asombolo was getting nicely into the swing of things, his tongue deep in Petra's mouth when the phone pealed out. Automatically, he jerked away to pick it up, but Petra bit his tongue viciously, and he squealed with pain.

'Remember how much you love me!' she hissed. 'Who gives a fuck about the phone?'

Asombolo was unhappy. He recollected perfectly his all too recent declaration of affection, but he also had an unpleasant memory of what had happened when he had last ignored a phone call because he was fully occupied with Petra.

'It might be Milos,' he ventured.

'Nonsense!' she contradicted. 'Milos is a gentleman and he would not call when we were in the sack.'

Another painful nip on his tongue served to underline her determination that she would yield to nobody, and Asombolo, though ill at ease, submitted. It was hard to concentrate with the phone demanding his attention, but after a few minutes, it stopped. Petra had inserted her finger up his arse, and he was squirming delightedly, when the two-tone bell of the phone resumed its racket. The increased pressure of her finger warned him that a renewed attempt to take the phone would result in his requiring at least intermediate surgery. Resolutely shutting his ears to the clamour, he set about fucking her. Once he had penetrated her, they melted together and everything was so sublime that they did not even notice the moment when the phone stopped ringing. However, they did notice when somebody began hammering on the bedroom door.

'Don't you dare to move,' Petra threatened.

'Monsieur Asombolo, please, this is urgent,' came a voice from the corridor.

It was no use. Casanova himself would have been rendered sexless. With a leap like a frightened gazelle, Asombolo disentangled himself from Petra, grabbed a towel which he draped around his loins, and went to the door.

Outside there stood not a humble messenger boy, but one of the receptionists, who handed a piece of paper to Asombolo.

'I was taking a shower,' explained the Chief Minister.

'Come back, you fucking bastard!' shrieked Petra.

The receptionist wore a wooden expression and looked right through Asombolo, as if to register that he had not noticed that the African's body was perfectly dry, or that there was a screaming nude woman on the bed.

'If you read the message, you will see why we felt it necessary to disturb you, sir,' said the receptionist.

'Imperative that you are on the 14.30 Swissair flight to Zurich. You will be met at airport – Ben,' were the words written on the paper.

'But that is in one hour,' Asombolo cried in dismay.

'I'll bite off your ugly great prick and stuff it down your throat,' Petra promised.

The receptionist continued his policy of turning a blind eye and a deaf ear to the incensed lady. 'We could book you on to the flight while you are getting dressed and have a taxi waiting for you in five minutes.'

'Please, do that,' Asombolo entreated.

'Would you want one seat or two?' asked the tactful clerk.

'You impotent lump of horse shit!' Petra interposed.

'Two. And have my bill ready,' Asombolo told the receptionist, and silently pledged to leave the man a sovereign-sized tip. To Petra he called, 'Get your clothes on in just two minutes or you will be walking home.'

Shortly after the last of the ACE Office Cleaning and Decontamination Company vans had vanished from the centre of Zurich, one of them sped into the waiting area at the airport. Max leaped out, just in time to intercept Asombolo and Petra. When they emerged from the terminal building, the Chief Minister erupted in an outburst of indignation. He could tolerate being dragged from his bed of love and ordered in and out of Geneva at a moment's notice, but to be transported across the city in a tradesman's van, that was insupportable.

'Sorry, your excellency,' chirped Max impenitently, 'but we have been out on a job, and the Rolls has been repossessed by the finance company.'

At about the same time, Sandra opened her eyes and looked up into the face of Ben the Bear. Her head throbbed, her eyes stung and her mouth felt as if she had eaten a carpet.

'Had a good sleep?' enquired Ben.

She groaned. The recollection of the horror of the orgy in the temple flooded back. For a second, she thought that she had been rescued: then she remembered Ben trapping her and handing her over to Isis, Ben tricking Louis and their imprisonment on the *Firebird*, Ben promising to protect her and the Golden Phallus, and Ben pocketing Grunwald's cheque.

'Now what?' she asked listlessly. 'Are you shipping us out to Salamba?'

'Whatever would give you that idea?' Ben said. 'Don't you like Zurich?'

'I think that Uncle is returning to the land of the living,' called one of Ben's assistants.

Sandra raised herself on one elbow and surveyed the scene. She was reclining on a sofa in some sort of office. Louis Halevy was sprawled in an easy chair, facing a desk. His eyes were closed, but he was stirring faintly.

'Is he all right?' asked Sandra in alarm.

'Perfectly,' Ben replied. 'He will have a bit of a hangover, but probably no worse than yours. Mind you, he did give us something of a problem. You two were glued together so hard that David here wanted to use a crowbar to prise you apart. I would have expected a seemly detumescence from Uncle when he took his nap, but he stayed as erect as a guardsman on parade.'

'We had to cool his ardour by dribbling ice-cold water over his somewhat public private parts,' David informed her.

With a start, she realized that neither she nor the recumbent professor were wearing a stitch of clothing, but that they had preserved a semblance of modesty since bath towels had been thrown over them. She pulled her towel protectively around her: Ben noted her action and apologized.

'I am sorry that your dress is so informal, but we did not have the time to get you clothed. That temple was an unhealthy location.'

'Where am I?' Such was Halevy's initial contribution to the conversation.

'Welcome to the offices of the ACE Office Cleaning and Decontamination Company,' declaimed David. 'Would you like a guided tour of the premises?'

'Steady on!' Ben protested. 'No man with a head like he must have should be subjected to such heartless heartiness. Why don't you be the Good Samaritan and fetch our two guests a drink?'

'Just plain water for me,' said Sandra.

'Very sensible,' Ben concurred.

At the sound of Sandra's voice, Halevy had pulled himself up to a sitting position and he gazed at her in obvious concern. Any explanation of what had happened to them was delayed by the arrival of David with a report of the police activity at the bank.

'When they found the tunnel from the tobacconist's shop and realized that it led directly into the vaults of the bank, they had a whole litter of kittens. They were sure that the biggest robbery the world has ever seen had been perpetrated, but then they were told that absolutely nothing was missing. As if that were not baffling enough for our plodding sleuths, they see with their own eyes that whoever it was that had broken into the premises had left behind a bloody great golden idol. The bank manager disclaims any knowledge of the object. The last I heard was that the chief of the city police had booked an appointment with a psychiatrist.'

Max burst into the room, leading Asombolo and Petra.

'I think that you and the lady are already well acquainted,' Ben said to Sandra and Halevy. 'May I introduce you to the Chief Minister of Salamba.'

'So you are intending to hijack us to Salamba,' accused Halevy.

'But she is not the woman,' complained Asombolo, pointing at Sandra. 'We have paid for Isis, not for some second-rate substitute.'

'That is no way to refer to one of my close associates,' Ben rebuked him. 'I have no intention of shipping out this lady or her friend anywhere. Isis, along with all her acolytes, is upstairs in our store room, safely locked in and peacefully sleeping off the effects of the boisterous festivities. You have paid for Isis, you get Isis. I think that it will be helpful if Max brings in the body of our somnolent banker. And David, it would be a kind act if you were to go and buy some clothes for Professor Halevy and Miss Mitchell.'

The two men went out and Max returned a few minutes later, escorting Josef Grunwald, still resplendent in his orgy costume. This was a strange affair, since when he had gone to a theatrical costumier to hire Egyptian dress, he had found that all the available outfits had been taken, presumably by other devotees of Isis who wanted to enter into the spirit of their gala. So, as the nearest approximation, he had taken a Roman toga, together with accessories, having been assured by the proprietor of the establishment that nobody would spot the discrepancy.

'I suppose that you have come to bury Caesar, not to praise him,' Ben commented sadly.

The banker, still rather green round the gills, made a pathetic effort to look dignified, but his now rather soiled toga was not the most flattering garment for his portly figure, and his garland of plastic laurel leaves hung limply over his bald head. With an effort, he summoned up the last tatters of his respectability.

'I demand an explanation of this outrage,' he spluttered to Ben.

'Which particular outrage?' his host asked innocently. 'You have quite a choice.'

'Where is Isis?' Grunwald demanded.

'She is in our store room, awaiting shipment to Salamba,' Ben said. He turned to Asombolo. 'And that will fulfil my contract with Milos.'

'But you cannot do that,' Grunwald protested. 'You took our money and now you betray us!'

'I beg your pardon,' Ben contradicted. 'I was never commissioned by you or anybody else to protect Isis. The ACE Office Cleaning and Decontamination Company has accepted a number of assignments, and it is my contention that every one of them has been fulfilled to the letter. I was paid by Isis to hand over to her Miss Mitchell and Professor Halevy, which I did when they were delivered to the barge *Firebird*. Once they had gone on board, my contract had been honoured. I had no obligation to keep them in her custody. In fact, quite the reverse, since I had agreed with Professor Halevy to protect the two of them and the Golden Phallus, another obligation which I have dealt with as promised. And as for you, Josef Grunwald, you ordered the delivery of the statue of Osiris to Cairo: you got it, while the Golden Phallus was handed over on the *Firebird*. It seems to me that you are guilty of gross ingratitude.'

Grunwald looked as if he were about to have a stroke. 'You will regret this trickery,' he shouted. 'You forget that my bank is a powerful institution. We shall hound you out of business and out of Switzerland.'

'Now I am very glad that you brought up the position of the bank,' Ben replied cordially. 'At this very minute, it is swarming with police who are most anxious to interview one of the members of the board of directors about the existence of a secret tunnel into the vaults. They are also most curious about a more than life-size golden statue which they have discovered. It is my understanding that they are puzzled at not being able to locate one single director. I could, of course, assist them on the last point, since all your colleagues are in the store room in even fancier dress than your own. I can also let them have the video recordings which were being made of the orgy of Isis. The directors, including yourself, are clearly recognizable. Shall I call the cops to come and collect the whole gang now?'

Grunwald considered. 'Perhaps I have been a little too hasty in condemning you. We ought to be able to come to some arrangement for old time's sake, don't you think?'

Ben nodded. 'How would you like it if I had you run home in one of our closed vans so that you can change into something more contemporary before exhibiting yourself?'

'Most kind of you.' Grunwald favoured Ben with a smile like a sick halibut. 'Of course, I shall have to think up something to explain the statue of Osiris.'

'Not at all,' Ben told him. 'It had been deposited in the bank by a customer, who is the rightful owner. Due to its size, it could not have been accommodated in the usual strong room, so you had this extra vault excavated, with a secret entrance for security. That was expensive, but once the work had been done, your bank would be able to look after other objects of great value which were jumbo-sized. As soon as the rest of your board have recovered and become aware of the existence of those video recordings, you can bet your life that they will back up your story.'

'The police might swallow it,' Grunwald said thoughtfully, 'but we shall have to produce a customer.'

'But you have one,' Ben smiled. 'I am sure that you remember that when I was hired to collect the statue from Salamba, you informed me that it was the intention of the bank to give the relic to a worthy museum or similar institution. And that is why you called in Professor

Halevy, to advise you. Waiting to take delivery of it is Professor Khalid of the National Museum of Egypt who I am sure will express his gratitude to the bank for the care with which they have guarded this priceless object.'

'But Khalid is in Paris and knows nothing about this,' Halevy put in.

'Sorry to contradict you, but he is here in Zurich,' said Ben. 'He came in response to the telegram which you sent him, or, to be more precise, which I sent him in your name.'

There was a stunned silence, as each of the clients of the ACE Office Cleaning and Decontamination Company assessed his or her situation.

Then Grunwald spoke. 'Can I have a drink?'

'And when do we take Isis?' Asombolo asked.

'I suggest that we put her in one of our vans directly after Professor Halevy has formally presented the statue to Khalid. And to prove that I am not mean, I intend to give President Milos a bonus in the person of Cleo Janis, with the compliments of the company and at no extra charge.'

It was Sandra who wound up the proceedings. Hoisting her towel stylishly around her, she crossed to where Ben was sitting and kissed him on the cheek.

'Oh admirable bear,' she hailed him. 'You really are James Super-Bond.'

'And can I enrol you as Jane Bond?' he queried.

'Maybe,' she conceded.

'Would you have a job for me too?' piped up Petra.

'But what about your studies at the university?' asked Halevy.

Petra grimaced. 'I guess I am cut out for a more active life. You know I have never been so happy as I was when I was fighting in the jungle with Milos and his guerrillas.'

'And you would not mind being back with him,' Halevy commented.

'Well now,' Ben told her. 'In view of the amount of work which has been flooding in recently, I could do with some reinforcements. Why don't I put you on probation and give you something to do and see how you get along?'

Petra looked at him eagerly.

'How about your accompanying the Chief Minister together with his two prisoners to Ibari. You could keep an eye on them to make sure that they do not get up to any of their tricks, ride shotgun, as it were.'

Sandra and Halevy repressed their smiles at the phrase and Petra was so delighted that another kiss was planted on Ben's cheek. The proceedings were interrupted by the return of David from his shopping expedition. He was promptly sent off again, this time to convey Grunwald to his home. Everybody else went upstairs to scrutinize the flotsam of humanity which had been washed up in the store room, modestly leaving Sandra and Louis Halevy to put on their newly-acquired clothes. Isis was sitting on her own, staring vacantly into space, and she ignored the arrival of all the party except Ben.

'Many men have lied to me with words from their mouths, but you have lied with all your body,' she said in a low, bitter voice.

She turned away from him, and for once the bear made no reply.

When they rejoined Halevy and Sandra, Ben addressed the Egyptologist. 'This evening, we shall join Khalid in the bank vault for a formal handing over of the statue of Osiris. The Golden Phallus has been removed, but is perfectly safe. I want to ask you to present the statue as it is now, without the Phallus. I promise that I shall account to you for that object afterwards, but there is a good and compelling reason why it should not be included in tonight's ceremony.'

Halevy looked quizzically at him. 'I suppose that this is one more of your mystifications, Ben?'

'I think that you should do as he asks,' Sandra said. 'You do trust him, don't you?' she added mischievously.

'Well, the Golden Phallus has not been definitely promised to Khalid,' said Halevy pensively. 'If you consider it to be so important, I agree. But I reserve the right to present it to him later.'

Ben nodded assent. 'The Egyptians are not doing badly in any case, are they? Surely most statues of that style are dongless?'

The actual presentation was a brief, unspectacular business. The police, having been assured of the right of Halevy to dispose of the object and their doubts about the newly-discovered vault having been allayed by Grunwald, raised no objections to the party meeting there, along with selected press and camera men, under strict security, of course. Both professors made short statements about the uniqueness of the statue, there were a few desultory questions, and then everybody went off, Khalid to start making arrangements for the shipping of the statue, the representatives of the media to work on the next story, and Ben, Sandra and Halevy to have a farewell dinner in a private club of which Ben was a member.

'Well,' said Halevy, when they had finished their meal, 'when are you going to reveal to us why you were so insistent that I should not hand over the Golden Phallus?'

'My reason was that I did not want to expose you to the risk of being denounced as a fraud.'

'What do you mean by that?' Halevy bristled with indignation.

'Think, both of you,' Ben told them. 'Isn't there another question which you ought to have asked me, in particular about your rescue?'

Halevy looked baffled. Sandra replied, 'I think I know what you are getting at. How did you know where to find us before it was too late. Is that the question?'

'Well done, Jane Bond. Let me show you something.'

Ben walked over to the cloakroom and returned, carrying the familiar cardboard box. He opened it and withdrew the great rod of gold which he handed to Halevy.

'Please examine this and let me have your informed opinion on its authenticity,' he said.

Halevy handled it carefully for a minute. Then his expression grew grim.

'This is not the Golden Phallus which I entrusted to you. It is a clever modern imitation. Would you mind telling me what you have done with the original?'

'It is a great deal more clever than you realize,' Ben told him. And taking back the strange object, he pointed out a hairline where the metal had been joined.

'I needed to see the real thing and have its exact dimensions and weight and to take those photographs in the bank, so that this thing could be fabricated. Since Isis would not disclose where her infernal temple was, I had to have a way of tracking her. Inside this fake phallus there is a miniature transmitter: it is a rather exotic bug, nothing more, but gold plated and weighted to make it indistinguishable from the original at a casual glance even by you, let alone by someone who had never seen the real thing. I certainly did not want you handing this over to Khalid, who would sooner or later have tumbled to it and would have accused you of every kind of trickery.'

'And the original?'

'Where you always kept it, Louis, safe and sound in your safe deposit box in your bank. It never left there. While you were signing the forms for withdrawing it, I slipped it back in the safe deposit instead of my phoney jewels.'

Halevy shook his head in bewilderment.

Sandra wheeled on Ben. 'Do you mean to tell us that all the time that we were being subjected to every kind of torment on that bloody boat and later in the temple, you were aware of exactly where we were and could have pulled us out at any time?'

'That's right. But I wanted to finish the Isis racket for ever, and that meant rounding all of them up in their hidden temple, so you have to go right through with the game to the end. You were never in mortal danger, you know, because Isis wanted to preserve you for the final immolation in front of the altar of Osiris.'

'You knew that, but we didn't,' Sandra pointed out angrily. 'Why didn't you let us know? Both of us were sure that you had betrayed us: we went through hell!'

'If you had been aware of what was going on, you would never have managed to deceive Isis and Drummond. I had no confidence in your abilities as actors and if you had made one false move, then you would have been killed on the spot. It was essential for your safety that you remained genuinely scared out of your wits.'

'You cold-blooded, calculating bastard,' she gasped.

'But he was quite right, dear,' Halevy admitted. 'Still, you know, it is not at all pleasant being live bait, Ben.'

'Bears play rough,' Ben grinned. 'Have another brandy.'

# 15
## *Taken to the Cleaners*

Early the following morning, Ben and his staff were busy dispersing the rank and file disciples of Isis. A night on the concrete floor of a draughty store room, wearing only the tatters of their fancy costumes and without food, had had a depressing effect on them, and there was no trace remaining of their former religious zeal. They were given a simple breakfast and each of them was issued with a pair of jeans, a shirt, ten Swiss francs – and a bicycle.

'Go home, you indescribable bunch of weirdos, and think yourselves lucky that we are not turning you over to the police,' thundered Ben. 'Now, beat it!'

An overweight girl complained that she would have to pedal all the way to Berlin.

'But just think what a sensational figure you will have when you get there,' David told her by way of consolation.

A freckled young man looked even unhappier than his colleagues. He pointed at his bicycle. 'How the heck do you expect me to get home on this thing? I live in Charleston, South Carolina.'

'When you get to the coast, trade it in for a canoe,' suggested Max, helpful as ever.

Eventually, the last of them had been shooed away. Isis remained, together with Cleo Janis and Andrew Drummond. The two women were taken, heavily escorted, to the airfield where Asombolo's pilot shepherded them to a waiting plane without their being bothered with such formalities as customs and border police controls. He explained to the Chief Minister that because most of the airfield was in France, not Switzerland, he had been able to devise a system by which the French officials presumed that they had passed through the Swiss checks and the Swiss were under the impression that they had been covered by the French. Apparently the payment of a certain amount of money ensured that this misapprehension persisted. Ben avoided coming into contact with Isis before she left; he had no stomach for fond farewells, but occupied himself with the disposal of Andrew Drummond.

'I must get back to my practice,' the doctor blustered. 'There are people who are in need of my skill and experience.'

Ben nodded, but his expression was bleak. 'I have checked up and although you are undoubtedly a sadistic criminal, it seems that you have quite an impressive medical reputation. However, you have absented yourself from your work whenever it suited you or Isis, so I have planned a spell of corrective treatment for you before you are set free to resume your career.'

'Now, look here, let's be reasonable,' Drummond objected.

Ben silenced him. 'The Italian police have discovered the body of a young woman in an abandoned building which used to be a clinic in the outskirts of Rome. She had been extensively drugged and then murdered. Interpol are looking for a man and a woman who were seen there. Would you like to help the police with their investigations?'

Drummond shrugged his shoulders. 'Without a positive identification, they could not prove anything.'

'There would be fingerprints,' Ben pointed out. 'And some of the local hoods who were used as guards might be persuaded to remember faces.'

Like a good chess player who finds himself one move away from being checkmated, Drummond conceded gracefully.

An hour later, one of the ubiquitous vans belonging to the ACE Office Cleaning and Decontamination Company drew up beside a jetty on the river Rhine in Basle. Andrew Drummond, now dressed in a pair of heavy denim trousers and a seaman's jersey, climbed out and, together with Ben and Max, walked over to where the barge, *Firebird*, having been loaded with a cargo for Rotterdam, was being prepared for its return journey. The three men clambered on board where they were met by the Grand Duke Alexei and Frank.

The master of the vessel remembered Drummond and eyed him enquiringly.

'Mr Drummond has been advised to take a sea voyage for his health,' Ben explained, 'but we felt that a few trips up and down the Rhine would serve just as well. He has requested that he should not be offered special treatment of any kind, but should be considered as simply one of your crew.'

'What made him pick *Firebird*?' Frank asked. His face registered suspicion and hostility.

'But it is obvious,' bubbled the Grank Duke. 'This one, he operated on my leg after the disastrous *entrechat*, he is crazy on the ballet, no? He wants to put on the works of my great uncle, Vladimir, yes? So, all day, when he is not working, we talk about the ballerinas of the Bolshoi and how I got Diaghilev drunk, but that one he still did not produce Vladimir's ballet in Monte Carlo and how Balanchine really had a wooden leg when he danced Casse Noisette in St Petersburg and – '

'Oh no, he bloody well won't!' Frank interrupted vehemently. 'I'll keep the bastard working through the day till his balls fall off.'

'No matter,' beamed the amiable skipper. 'At night, he will be third horse. At last, I drive the troika!'

The grand duke was ecstatic, and he kissed Ben and Max effusively to express his gratitude.

'And if you attempt to jump ship, there will be Interpol agents on top of you before you can get your arse clear of the river,' Ben promised the morose ship's doctor by way of farewell.

'Bon voyage,' called Max.

In Ibari, Milos received his Chief Minister and Petra, the other two women remaining outside under armed guard. When he caught sight of Petra, his face creased into a great smile.

'Why, hallo, this is a surprise!' he exclaimed. 'It's been ages since you ran out on me.'

But Petra knew how to retaliate. 'Sandra sends her love,' she said with a mean smile.

'God, how I suffered for that woman!' Milos sighed. 'But that's all in the past. You are looking good.' There was that old glint in his eyes which Petra remembered from their days and nights together in the jungle.

Asombolo considered that it was time to get back to business. 'I have brought you back the woman, Isis, as you ordered. And Cleo Janis is with her. I am sure that you will want to see them now.' He gestured to Petra to make herself scarce, but she ignored him and stood her ground.

If Asombolo expected congratulations on the success of his mission, he was doomed to bitter disappointment.

'You certainly took your time, didn't you,' scowled the President. 'And the Minister of the Finance found out how much you spent on your jaunt and had to be given oxygen. So, you will have to pay your own expenses.'

The Chief Minister looked glum but raised no objection. As he and the Minister of Finance were partners in certain fund-raising activities, he was sure that he would be spared any lasting financial embarrassment. However, he did not think that Milos should have bawled him out in front of Petra: it wounded his pride. He saw with annoyance that she was actually laughing at him.

'Come with me,' Milos said to Petra. 'We have a lot to talk about.'

She went to him. There was a provocative roll to her hips which revived desire in Asombolo. He could swear that she was licking her lips as she took Milos's arm.

She looked back over her shoulder with a smile. 'Good-bye,' she said, and walked out of Asombolo's life.

Isis and Cleo were also received warmly, although not by the President in person. With a sinking heart, Cleo recognized the low barracks to which they were led. And there to greet them bounded the big black sergeant.

'Great to have you back,' he roared. 'And with your friend, even better! You know what? We heard that you were here, so the boys drew lots: that's really democratic!'

'Don't tell me,' Cleo groaned. 'You are first?'

'That's right, lady. I am always first. Come right in. Say, what's your friend's name? She looks a real doll.'

'You had better call me Anna,' said the woman who for a few weeks had been Isis.

Ben accompanied Halevy and Sandra back to Paris and went with them to the bank where Halevy satisfied himself that the real Golden Phallus was, as Ben had assured him, still in his safe deposit box.

Ben pointed at the relic. 'Let me ask you something, Louis.' He spoke with unwonted seriousness. 'Do a lot of other people know of the existence of this monstrosity?'

'Quite a few have heard of the stories about it, but I don't suppose that there are many scholars who would stand up and say that they are sure that it is fact and not fiction. Why?'

'As long as there is a Golden Phallus, you will have new pretenders to the mantle of Isis,' Ben answered. 'And we have seen that means people who are prepared even to kill to attain the power that they believe is embodied inside that thing. Destroy it.'

'What? After all we have gone through!' Halevy was horrified.

'If it had not existed, you would not have had to go through all that trouble, would you? And look, it is not exactly a thing of beauty, is it?'

All the Professor's academic instincts were against a wilful act of destruction, but Sandra joined in. 'Do it, Louis. The damned thing is evil.'

And so the Golden Phallus of Osiris was melted down in a furnace and the gold converted into ingots which were sold. The money which it raised was sent by Halevy to Khalid as a bequest to the National Museum in Cairo. 'I suggest,' he wrote, 'that you use it to increase the security on the statue of Osiris.'

There was one other souvenir of their exploits, a cedar wood casket containing various papers and a faded piece of papyrus. Halevy carefully examined these objects, and he told Sandra and Ben the results of his analysis.

'The casket is a nice piece of work,' he commented. 'It is not an artefact of which I have any precise knowledge, but I have consulted some specialists, colleagues at the Sorbonne. They judge it to be about twenty years old and probably manufactured in Portugal, although they do not rule out the possibility of it originating in Hong Kong. The papers are rubbish.'

'But what about the papyrus? That is a genuine relic from ancient Egypt, isn't it?' Sandra demanded.

'Yes, indeed,' Halevy assented. 'It is a singular document. I have studied it extensively.'

'Could you translate it? What does it mean?'

Sandra's curiosity was understandable in view of the mysterious erotic influence that the papyrus in the hands of the priestess had exerted over so many men and women.

'It is a recipe for making a sort of pudding out of barley and goat meat. Not particularly appetizing, but it is perhaps the earliest fragment of a cookery book to have been discovered. Quite remarkable,' Halevy said, with academic smugness.

'But that's impossible!' Sandra exploded. 'How could Isis weave her spells with a primitive gourmet's guide?'

'I assure you that there is no doubt over the meaning of the characters.' Halevy was not going to let anybody dispute the soundness of his scholarship. 'I suppose you can hypnotize people with any old nonsense, once they are in a receptive frame of mind.'

'You may not be able to fool all the people all the time,' Ben stated cynically, 'but you can fool a hell of a lot of them, for a hell of a lot of the time.'

Later that evening, Ben announced that he would be going back to Zurich next morning.

'There are a lot of jobs waiting for me to deal with, and I rather let things slide while everybody in the company concentrated on settling this affair.'

'We shall miss you, shan't we, Sandra?' said Halevy.

'I am sure that you will, Louis, darling. But I thought that I might help Ben to clear up some of this backlog of work. After all, we are largely responsible for it being there. That is, if there is still a vacancy for a part-time Jane Bond,' she asked Ben tentatively.

'Welcome to the firm,' he said with a broad grin.

'But do you mean that you are leaving me?' cried Halevy.

'You knew that I was not going to stay indefinitely. I only hung on because you were in danger, and Petra was not with you.'

Halevy looked so distressed that she felt quite guilty. 'I'll come and see you. Honestly,' she tried to comfort him.

When the two of them had departed, Halevy reflected. As soon as he had possession of the Golden Phallus of Osiris, two beautiful women had stayed with him, and how they had made love! Now that the Phallus was no more, Petra had left him for Milos, and Sandra was going away with Ben. Despite his scepticism, he could not help asking himself as he prepared to go to bed alone – coincidence or magic?

THE END